Christina Cornwell has four children and lives in Poole Dorset with her beloved dog, Tinkerbell. She worked for the local authority for several years before retiring, plus many other jobs over the years. Her main hobby now is her garden and growing flowers and long walks with Tinkerbell.

With thanks to Paul Moore and his lovely family.

In the FISH PLACE in Weymouth for feeding my imagination with their wonderful fish and chips and friendships.

Christina Cornwell

MAGNET TO MURDER

AUSTIN MACAULEY PUBLISHERS™
LONDON * CAMBRIDGE * NEW YORK * SHARJAH

A CIP catalogue record for this title is available from the British Library.

ISBN 9781398499485 (Paperback)
ISBN 9781398499492 (ePub e-book)

www.austinmacauley.co.uk

First Published 2024
Austin Macauley Publishers Ltd®
1 Canada Square
Canary Wharf
London
E14 5AA

Georgina and Harriet

The village bus jolted slowly along the narrow road, Harriet sighed and wondered how long it would take to get home. Her feet were killing her, she had mistakenly worn a new pair of shoes, to wander round Palmouth, shopping.

A tractor pulled out in front of the bus with a trailer loaded with bales of straw. The driver seemed totally unaware of the bus behind and took his time. After a mile or so, Harriet's attention was taken by a conversation taking place, by the two women sitting behind her.

'Well, I don't know what to do about Reg, I am sure he is up to something, but don't know how to prove it.'

'Oh, Gloria I don't know what to think, his behaviour is very suspicious,' the other woman replied.

'It's worrying me sick, I don't care what it costs, I need to know. I will kill him if I find he is making a fool of me.'

Without thinking, Harriet rummaged in her bag and pulled out a card. She turned round and offered the card to one of the women.

'Perhaps you would find this useful, they are very good.'

The bus was just pulling up at Harriet's bus stop, she collected her bags, smiled at the two women and got off the bus.

Once indoors, with her shoes thankfully off and a cup of tea in her hand, she began to panic.

'Bugger, what have I done?'

She picked the phone up and dialled Georgina's number.

Georgina Wright and Harriet Holt lived in a small village called, Gorlstone. On the outskirts of the coastal town of Palmouth.

They had met in the office of the local council, over 20 years ago, where they both worked, and had become friends.

Harriet had given up her job six years ago and had moved to Kent, to be near her husband's family. The two women had kept in contact over the years. Georgina had visited Harriet, with her husband, on several occasions. Their husbands both enjoyed a game of golf and the girls enjoyed catching up with all the gossip, visiting local charity and antique shops.

A year ago, Harriet's husband Geoff died. Most of her husband's family had also passed away, so Harriet decided to move back to the Palmouth area, once she had sold her house. She had been lucky to find a house in Gorlstone, the same small village as Georgina, who was delighted to have her old pal back. Georgina had also retired from the council and with her friend now back, hoped to spend some girlie time together with Harriet.

Sadly, within a few months of Harriet's return to Gorlstone, Georgina's husband died, and Harriet was glad to be there for her friend.

Gorlstone was a one street village, with a couple of lanes leading to the surrounding countryside.

There were decorative trees planted on either side of the main street. The residents took great pride in their front gardens and Gorlstone often won prizes in the best kept village competitions.

The village shop was still thriving and was at the centre of the village. The post office counter had been taken away some time ago, but the shop was convenient for residents, for their groceries and newspapers. It was also the best way to keep up with the local gossip. There was even a couple of chairs outside, to sit and have a chat.

Georgina lived in a detached three-bedroomed bungalow in Cherry Lane, one of the lanes off the main road. Her house looked out over the arable fields, and was just 50 yards from the main street. Harriet had bought a Victorian semi, behind what was the old village bakery, on Ashdown Lane. Which also led off the main street but on the opposite side of the street. All they had to do was walk up their respective lane, and cross the main street to visit each other.

Fortunately, a by-pass had been built in the seventies and traffic was light through the village, so the village was fairly quiet with a mainly ageing population.

Georgina was 63 and Harriet 65 years old, but both refused to be old. Geriatric teenagers they jokingly called themselves. They had comforted each other when they had lost their husbands and spent at least a couple of days a week, 'doing things'.

How to Get Rich or Arrested

Ignorance of the Law excuses no man.

– John Selden

They frequently discussed money-making projects, although they were both reasonably well off, boredom was their enemy.

Georgina picked the ringing phone up.

'Georgie, thank God you are in. I think I have done something daft.' Harriet was in panic mode!

'What's new, what have you done now?'

Georgina was quite used to Harry's panics.

'Well, you remember the cards I made, when we joked about becoming private detectives?'

Georgina laughed. 'When we thought we could be the next Miss Marple? Another of your dopey ideas!'

Harriet sighed and laughed.

'l heard these women talking about one of their husbands being a naughty boy. So, I gave them one of those cards I made, I don't know what came over me, a bloody mad moment!'

'What happens if they phone? Who's telephone number is on the card?' Georgina asked.

'Um, your mobile and my mobile!'

'Well Miss Marple, let's hope they lose the card, but what do we do if they phone?'

'Panic, comes to mind. Or we could say we were already on a case and too busy.'

'Oh really! What are we looking for, Lord Lucan?'

Just then, Harriet's mobile started to ring.

'Oh Georgie, what if it's her? Bloody hell, why am I such an idiot?'

Georgina laughed 'Why change the habits of a lifetime, just answer the phone, probably some twit trying to sell you their services for the car accident you haven't had!'

Georgina and Harriet had remained firm friends and enjoyed each other's company. Same sense of humour and interests. Harriet was the one who had the wild ideas and Georgina was 'the sensible one', they always laughingly said.

They met most days, had coffee and patrolled the charity shops, among other things.

'What we need, is an aim in life. Other people seem to find a way to make money and have some fun at the same time,' Harriet had said. Georgina agreed and they had discussed several ideas, some crazy, like the Miss Marple idea.

But the idea had been binned, as probably, they realised they would have to be registered or something, have insurance, plus the fact neither of them had any experience, apart from being very nosey!

Last Spring, they had scoured the charity shops for ladies' hats, taken them home, tarted them up and put them on E-bay a few weeks, before Ascot.

The hats had sold like hot cakes. After Ascot week, the rush slowed and they sold one here and there.

Then the good old Post Office put the boot in and raised postage charges and the closure of the village post office complicated the situation, so that idea 'bit the dust'.

The next idea wasn't long in coming.

They tried to make bikinis. But as neither was good at dress making, the end results were not a success.

When they tried on their efforts, they decided the bikinis would make better catapults, or some would need ladies with different size breasts. But at least they had a good laugh over their efforts.

They then got a job delivering parcels. Harriet was the driver, Georgina the deliverer. Their sense of direction was a problem, and they spent more time lost in some out of the way place, or occasionally in a field, swearing at the Sat Nav.

The 'beware of the dog' signs didn't bother Harriet, but Georgie wouldn't venture through those gates. Mostly the signs were an anti-burglar device, but Georgina wouldn't take the risk, so Harriet would disappear through the gates and had often got licked to death by a drooling Labrador. A couple of times Harriet had emerged rather sharpish with a growling monster hanging onto her coat.

After getting soaked with rain and arriving back to their homes in the dark, most days, and Harriet running out of coats without holes, they had thrown in the towel.

The private detective idea was more of a joke than a reality. They had joked about disguises and hiding in bushes. They had laughed over the whole idea, but never considered the project seriously.

Harriet read a lot of crime novels, and the Miss Marple, Agatha Rasen idea had seemed quite a lark.

And Harriet had designed a business card offering enquiry agent services, as a joke, and had put it into her handbag to show Georgina. The card had stayed in Harriet's bag for several months, now through a moment of madness she had offered it to the woman on the bus.

An Amusing Afternoon

A few days later, the ladies were sitting by the ornamental pond in the garden centre where they liked to lunch. Harriet's mobile phone started to ring. As per usual, her mobile was at the bottom of her capacious handbag. By the time she had rummaged through the detritus in her bag, the ringing had stopped.

One voice mail message had been left, 'Can't be anything important, I will listen to it later.'

As they sat in the sunshine, with their cream tea, the table next to them was initially vacant. As the two women talked, a large younger woman had come and sat down. The chairs were quite spindly metal affairs and not huge in the seat area, which was different to the female who had parked her oversize buttocks onto the chair.

Georgina looked at Harriet.

The woman's companion then came out of the café, bearing a tray filled with four enormous cream cakes and coffees. This lady was even heftier than the first. Harriet had tried not to watch, as the woman placed herself precariously onto the small chair.

Now it would have been normal for Harriet and Georgina to have ignored the other persons having snacks, but it became obvious that their two neighbours had wanted everyone to hear their conversation. They both had American accents, with the volume on high.

The conversation had been regarding breast implants! Just what was needed when eating cream cakes!

The larger lady was extremely well endowed in that department, in fact her bosoms had rested on the table, next to the plate of cakes, and had virtually escaped from the cleavage area of the strappy dress.

The little dog that belonged to the owner of the garden centre had trotted over, Harriet gave him a pat. He then went over to the next table and sniffed the large woman's legs and decided he liked the smell of the cream cakes. The larger woman tried to shoo him away, but he wasn't having it and persisted in his inspection of both the women's legs.

'Can you remove your dawg.' One of the women had said very loudly, looking at Harriet.

'No,'—she was going to say that the dog wasn't hers, but the big wobbling mountain of flesh had leapt up from her miniscule seat and bore down on Harriet and Georgina's table.

'I told you to take this smelly creature away,' The woman bawled.

As she had got up from her chair, one of the cream cakes had been knocked off the plate by the swinging breast. The little dog thought it was Christmas and picked up the cake and beat a hasty retreat.

Unfortunately, a big dollop of cream had been left on the patio, and as the woman stepped towards Georgina and Harriet, she slid across the stone slabs towards the pond.

Both Harriet and Georgina closed their eyes, expecting a large splash. No-one moved, and fortunately for the woman, her friend had leapt to her assistance, also sliding on the pile of cream, resulting in a heap of buttocks and other body parts sprawled at the edge of the pond.

Both women had untangled themselves and with as much dignity as they could muster, and picked up their bags and left the garden. Harriet and Georgina and the other persons sitting around the pond had all tried very hard not to laugh. Harriet and Georgina had laughed all the way home.

This incident, and the following giggles had taken all thoughts of the business card problem right out of their minds.

Panic Mode

That same evening, after Emmerdale, Harriet remembered the voice mail.

She wasn't too clever at using her mobile. She could never remember which buttons to press to retrieve her messages, but after a few minutes she got there.

Harriet listened horrified.

'Hello, my name is Gloria Partland. I was given your card by a woman on a bus. I think my husband is having an affair. Please can you tell me what your charges are, as I want someone to follow him for me.'

Harriet thought for a minute, then dialled the number that Gloria had left. The phone just rang and eventually went to the answer machine. Harriet was rather relieved, but decided to leave a message.

'Thank for calling, Mrs Partland. The investigators are out of the office at the moment, I will pass your number and message on to them, and get them to call you back,' she said in a squeaky voice.

'Flippin heck,' thought Harriet.

Harriet threw on her coat and left her house, carefully locking the door behind her.

'Oh, damn I should have brought my torch.'

There wasn't any light on her pathway, but once she reached the road, there was some light from the street light, just along the road.

She reached Georgina's bungalow and ran up the path and rang the bell. Georgina locked her door when it got dark, but she had a light outside her front door that came on if anyone approached her door.

Georgina opened her door, after Harriet shouted that it was her at the door, and let her friend in.

'Now what is so important, that gets you away from your knitting, at this time of night?' Georgina asked.

'That woman phoned, who I gave the card to. She wants us to follow her husband and wants to know how much we charge.'

Harriet expected an explosion from Georgina, but she only laughed and walked into her kitchen.

'Well Miss Marple, you've really done it this time. Let's find out the going rate, and double it, and then see if she is still interested. That should put her off! Now I was just going to make some hot chocolate, have one with me before you go back home.'

The next morning, Harriet looked through the yellow pages to find a contact number for firms of private investigators.

She phoned a couple, using a false name, explaining that she thought her husband was being unfaithful and asked what the charges were, if she were to employ them to find out what was going on.

Harriet was astonished at the figures quoted by each firm.

'Blimey, double that? That should put her off.' She thought.

After a strong cup of coffee, she telephoned Mrs Partland.

She adopted an affected voice, with a slight mixture of Loraine Kelly and Hyacynth Bucket!

She told Gloria the charges, trying to sound very confident, as though she was quite used to asking such high rates.

Gloria hesitated. 'Ok how do I pay you?'

Harriet was completely flabbergasted.

Suddenly her brain functioned. She asked Gloria for her address and told her that she would receive an application form in the post. Told her to give as much detail as she could about her husband's habits, car registration and include a recent photograph of her husband.

'The return address will be enclosed for you to return the required documents. You pay a £50 cash deposit, which you will send with the form. You pay the balance when your report is ready.'

'Georgie will kill me,' she thought, as she put the phone down. But a tingle of excitement spread through her.

'I can always plead senile dementia when they arrest me, I can say I am Jane Marple or Inspector Columbo!'

Harriet had another coffer, cuddled her dog and then phoned Georgina to report on progress.

Reg and Gloria

Reg and Gloria Partland lived in a small hamlet, a mile or so from Gorlstone.

As Gloria was putting her shopping away, she was thinking about her husband.

Reg worked as a benefits assessor for the local council. He had worked there for two years.

His driving school business had failed just before this. One of the large driving schools had set up in Palmouth. With their larger budget, they had flooded the town with advertising, and Reg had lost a lot of his customers.

He had been fortunate, his cousin, who worked in the human resources office for the council, had told him that the council were looking for benefit assessors. The advert was about to go into the Daily Clarion the following Thursday.

Reg had gone straight to the council offices in Palmouth and got an application form, filled it in straight away, and had been interviewed within a couple of weeks.

Apparently, two assessors had left suddenly, leaving the office desperately under staffed.

Reg had a degree in mathematics, and had always liked working with figures. But had taken over his father's driving school, when his dad had suffered a stroke, soon after Reg had achieved his degree.

His marriage, and the arrival of his son meant, he was stuck with the driving school for fifteen years. To please his ailing father, who had sadly passed away a year after the stroke, and to provide for his family.

The decision to ditch the driving school wasn't a hard one.

He had taken to the council job like a duck to water.

He really enjoyed it. At last, he was doing a job he really enjoyed.

Being a driving instructor had been a lonely occupation, just interaction with one person at a time. Sometimes he got very frustrated with the stupidity of his clients, especially the women and the cocky young men, who actually thought they knew better than him, or had delusions of being a racing driver.

Now he sat in an office with about ten other assessors and the banter between them was something that Reg enjoyed.

On a Friday night, several of his colleagues played darts in the pub. Reg started to go to the pub with them after the first few weeks of joining the office and soon became a member of the darts team and would go to the pub across the road for a pint and a game of darts or pool after work on Fridays.

Gloria had no objections to this, as on a Friday night she went to bingo in Palmarsh.

As Gloria was packing her frozen foods into her freezer, her thoughts were on Reg again.

His Friday night outings had started soon after he had begun working for the council. To start with, he had always been back home by the time Gloria had returned from bingo. But for the last six weeks, Reg had been at least an hour after Gloria had got indoors.

He had obviously had more than a couple of drinks each time, and had gone straight up to bed, often leaving Gloria downstairs watching the late-night film that they had previously watched together.

A fortnight ago, on a Thursday evening, about seven, Reg's mobile had rung. Reg was in the shower and he had left his phone in his suit jacket, which was hanging on the back of one of the dining room chairs.

Gloria had found the phone and was going to switch it off, as she was watching tv and the ringing was annoying her.

As she pulled the phone out of his pocket, the ads came on the tv and she saw that a text had come through on Reg's phone.

Without thinking, she had pressed the button to bring up the text and what she read, made her reach for the chair and sit.

'Hi Sexy, will be a bit late tomorrow night, hope your old lady not getting suspicious x Mandy.'

Gloria's first thought was to storm up to the bathroom and demand an explanation, but then she would have to admit that she had read his text.

Reg and Gloria had always shared everything, but had respected each other's privacy where phone calls and texts were concerned. Gloria had never been given reason to doubt her husband. They were childhood sweethearts and there were no secrets between them, or so Gloria thought.

She had not said anything to Reg.

The following evening, Gloria had left the Bingo Hall before the final games along with her best friend, Marion. She had confided in her friend and Marion has suggested driving to the Bull. As they were in Marion's car, they thought no one would recognise it as they drove into the pub car park.

As they entered the pub, Gloria felt very nervous, in case either Reg was not there or that he was with this 'Mandy' person.

Reg was surprised to see her. Marion lied and told Reg it was her birthday, so she had persuaded Gloria to go for a drink with her.

The two women were introduced to Reg's drinking partners, all male except one, who was the wife, of one of the men who also worked in the same office, but she was not called Mandy.

They had a couple of drinks then Marion drove Gloria back home.

Gloria had stewed over the text for the next week, still not saying anything to Reg.

The following Friday, Gloria thought, 'I can't turn up again at the Bull.' So she went off the bingo with Marion, although her mind did wander to the pub and the Mandy person.

That evening, when she got home, surprisingly Reg was already in the house, and dressed for bed. But he seemed distracted, and when Gloria asked him if he would like a cup of tea, he just snapped at her and went to bed.

Gloria made herself a cup of tea in the kitchen and was surprised to see the washing machine was on. She looked in the window of the machine and came to the conclusion that Reg had put his shirt into the machine along with his trousers that he had been wearing that evening.

After she had washed her tea cup, she went up to bed.

Reg was tucked down under the duvet and seemed to be asleep. One arm lay on top of the bed clothes.

As Gloria was getting undressed, she noticed the knuckles on his hand the skin was all red and there were abrasions on the back of his hand.

Because of the mood that he had gone to bed in, she decided to say nothing.

As she lay in bed, her imagination started to play with her mind. Had he had a fight with someone, perhaps this Mandy had a husband.

Gloria tossed and turned unable to settle, so she took one of her sleeping tablets, and eventually dropped off to sleep.

The next morning, being a Saturday, Reg always had a lie in. Gloria got up at eight as usual. After making a cup of tea, she emptied the washing machine and went into the garden to hang the clothes onto the line. As she shook out his shirt, a tie fell onto the path.

'Why on earth did he wash his tie as well?' Gloria thought.

A tingle of fear went through her mind, what on earth had he been up to?

An hour later, Reg came downstairs, looking really haggard.

Gloria decided not to question him and made him a cup of coffee, which was his morning poison.

'Think I've got a cold coming, have you got any aspirin?' Reg asked her.

Gloria found the tablets and a glass of water.

'I think I'll go back to bed for a while, I've got a stinker of a head ache.'

Reg then went back up the stairs. Gloria had tried to have a look at his hands, to see if the abrasions were on both of his hands, but he had managed to hold his hands under the table and obscured them from her eyes.

About eleven, Marion Jones knocked on Gloria's kitchen door.

'Put the kettle on Gloria, I am parched,' she said, as she sat herself down at the kitchen table.

'Have you heard about the body they have found in St. Thomas Street, last night in Palmarsh?'

Gloria's heart thumped so loudly she was sure Marion could hear it.

'No, I haven't been out yet, what happened?' She asked.

'Well, they were saying in Martindales paper shop in Gorlstone, that the police were called by one of their paper boys, who found the body. Rare shook up he was, poor little bugger.'

'Who was it, someone local?'

'Well, Margaret Sharples, you know her, the one who goes to bingo in her rollers, was outside talking to old Jim Talbot, and she said she thought it was Mandy Streatham's husband. She lives next door to the Streatham's, who live in those cottages, the next bus stop, along from Gorlstone village. The police were knocking on her front door this morning!'

That afternoon, Gloria had gone to Palmouth with Marion. They had discussed the 'Reg' problem on the bus as they were returning home. That was when, the old lady on the bus had given Gloria the card for the detective agency.

Reg had gone back to bed, but there was no way he could get off to sleep.

He looked at his bruised knuckles and wondered what on earth he had been thinking of. The two young men he had found trying to open his car door in the pub car park had been more of a handful than he had anticipated. He was not a violent man, but he had really lost his temper with the two thugs when they had taunted him.

'Piss off Grandad, we were just messing about.'

'You were trying to break into my car, you bastards.'

'Humph what would we want with a heap of junk like that.'

That was the 'red rag to the bull' moment with Reg. His car was his pride and joy, a Mark 2 Jaguar, even though it was over thirty years old, no-one insulted his car.

He had grabbed the bigger man by his jacket and threw him to the ground, the other man had tried to land a punch on Reg's head. Reg had boxed in the army, and dodged the flying fist and retaliated with an upper cut, that in sporting circumstances, any one would have been proud of.

The two thugs had enough and had run off into the roadway.

Now Reg's hand was sore and he felt ashamed that he had risen to the bait with the men. He certainly wasn't going to tell Gloria, as she hated fighting.

Reg realised that the fellows were probably after his pool cue which was lying on the back seat of his car, which was why he had gone back to the car from the pub.

Reg decided to get up. He went to the bathroom, put some antiseptic on his knuckles and wrapped a piece of crepe bandage around his hand.

Gloria noticed the bandage when she came back from her visit to town but said nothing.

'I shut my hand in the car door last night getting my pool cue out, what a wally I am!' Was the explanation Reg gave, when he saw Gloria looking at his bandaged hand.

Gloria wasn't too convinced that she had been told the truth about Reg's damaged hand. The 'Mandy thing' was still eating away at her, plus now the dead man in the town, with the added mention of the wife's name had added fuel to Gloria's worries.

Observation and Escape

Harriet typed up an application form on Sunday evening, making sure that the questions covered the necessary details about the husband. Before she could change her mind, she posted the application form to the address that Gloria had given her on the telephone call.

Harriet then went to post the letter, then walked on over to Georgina's house, to confess her sins.

Georgina laughed nervously when Harriet told her what she had done.

'You know there are laws about being an investigator. Think you have to register somewhere and get a licence.' Georgina had looked at Google and found out some information.

'Oh well, this will just have to be a one off, and let's hope we don't get found out.'

Three days later, the application form was returned with a small photo of the errant husband and fifty pounds. Gloria had also mentioned her fears regarding the injury to Reg's hand.

Harriet had given the return address for the form, as the empty old bakery at the front of her house.

The bakery was going to be turned into a charity shop very shortly and Harriet held the keys to the shop as she cleaned it for the owner.

Friday was the following day so the two women decided to visit the pub to observe their quarry.

They arrived at six-forty-five, and found themselves a seat as near to the dart board as was possible, so that they could not only see the players but also hear the conversations.

As they didn't know how long they would have to stay in the pub, they had decided to only drink coke.

At a few minutes to seven, the players began to arrive. Gloria's husband was the last player to arrive. His right hand was bandaged but he seemed in good spirits.

Harriet and Georgina were deep in conversation, seeming to take no interest in the darts team.

'How's the knuckles then Reg?' one of his friends asked.

'Not too bad mate. I would like to get my hands on those two thugs. I bet they go round all the car parks, looking for things left in cars.'

'Hopefully you can still throw a dart straight tonight. Your missus still no idea about next Saturday night?'

'No, when I saw your text, I thought blimey hope she doesn't see that, she will think I got some bird! Bloody Mandy, I shall call you that from now on!'

Both the men giggled like a couple of girls.

'Well Andy, don't think I fancy you even as Mandy. I got the two wigs and two frocks from Oxfam. She will have a laugh. I will make sure the lights are low for our first song and when we sing Happy birthday to her next Saturday, we will turn them up! Mandy and Candy will be revealed in all their glory or not, as the case may be.'

Harriet looked at Georgie and said very quietly, 'I think we have solved our first case Miss Marple!'

Georgina laughed and said, 'You are right Sherlock, let's go. But I need to spend a penny before we go.'

The two women made their way to the ladies. Nature satisfied, noses powdered and they were just coming out of the door to the toilet's, when Harriet back pedalled into Georgina.

'What you doing, you trod on my foot?'

Georgie rubbed her toes.

'Back inside quick, its Reg's wife and she is coming this way. She mustn't see me here.' Harriet went over to the window in the toilets and undid the catch on the sash window.

'You can't get out of there, you dope!'

'Give me a push, hurry. She doesn't know you.'

Georgie pushed Harriet up onto the window ledge, as Harriet raised the window.

Georgina started to laugh, 'I can see your drawers!'

'Bugger my drawers, push my other leg up.'

They could hear footsteps, and two women talking approaching the ladies toilets.

Georgie gave Harriet a mighty shove and she disappeared through the open window.

She quickly closed the window, just as two women walked into the toilets.

'Someone has been smoking in here, I had to open the window to get rid of the smoke,' she said to the two women, and with that walked out of the room.

She suddenly had a thought and wondered how high the window may have been from the ground below.

Visions of finding Harriet dangling from a tree or laying in the garden with broken limbs was going through her mind, as she hurried out of the front door of the pub.

A rather dishevelled Harriet was waiting outside. No broken bones, just muddy knees and a few scratches from a rather indignant climbing rose, that she had dislodged on her descent from the window, and a terrified pub cat that had been sitting on the grass below.

Once back in Harriet's car, they chuckled all the way home.

'Thought our days of window escapes were over, but it was fun.'

'We have solved the case though and what is nice we don't have to report anything bad, in fact we don't really want to spoil old Reg's surprise do we?' Georgina said.

'No, I will write the report and make sure it only gets back to Gloria next Saturday morning. I will tell her she has nothing to worry about and we found there is no woman called Mandy and suggest that if after the weekend she needs further help, she will have to go to another agency as we are closing for a vacation.'

'We can't make any further charge, can we? The only expense we had were for four cokes, and they have given me the wind! What next Sherlock?' Georgina said laughing.

'Well now we got to think up something else to do!' Harriet said.

Georgina cast her eyes skywards and hoped it didn't involve climbing out of more windows.

Harriet sent the report off to Gloria Partland, with a covering note stating that the expenses incurred had been minimal, so there was no further payment required. As an after-thought Harriet added, that if Mrs Partland would like to make a donation to Cancer Research, then she was sure they would be very appreciative.

They also decided to donate the fifty pounds deposit to the same cause. This salved Harriet's feelings of guilt over the whole thing.

If You Have Tears, Prepare to Shed Them Now

Shakespeare

A week later, Harriet was drinking tea in Georgina's kitchen.

'Well, we haven't heard from Gloria Partland, so I suppose that all ended happily,' Georgina said, as she refilled their cups.

'What now Sherlock? Back to making bras or have you got anymore brainwaves?' Harriet asked.

The two women laughed.

'Nearly time for The Chase on telly, and I've got a date with my ironing board tonight.' Harriet put down her cup. 'It gets dark so early now, I found that knitting pattern of bobble hats you wanted, I forgot to bring it over!'

'I will walk back over with you, as I found the bag of wool I had mislaid. I could make a start on making the hats tonight. Hang on a minute I will get my coat.'

Georgina put her coat and boots on, locked her door and followed Harriet down her front path.

As they walked up Cherry Lane, a person came running past the two women.

'Who was that?' Harriet asked.

'No idea, they seemed to be carrying something. Oh, look they are getting into that car that's parked just past my house.'

'Probably someone been to Martindales Stores. It's hard to park on the main road with the yellow lines now.'

By the time they got to Georgina's bungalow, the car had disappeared round the corner.

Georgina unlocked her door, Harriet stepped inside, while Georgina went into her lounge and picked up the knitting pattern for her friend.

'There you are, now you can have a knitting night.'

Georgina walked back to her front gate with Harriet.

'What's that noise?' Harriet said.

They could hear shouting and someone screaming.

'No idea, I can hear a siren, perhaps it's the cavalry coming.'

A police car sped through the village, but didn't stop.

'The screaming has stopped; do you want me to walk back to the main road with you?' Georgina asked.

'No, don't worry'

Just as Harriet stepped into the lane, someone came running past sobbing.

'That's young Janie. Hi Janie what's up love, can we help?'

The young woman stopped. She was looking up the lane, but turned her tear-stained face to Harriet.

'Oh Mrs Holt, I am sorry, I don't know what to do!'

Georgina came out of her gate, and put her arm round Janie and said, 'Come in and have a cup of tea with me and Harriet, love.'

Janie followed Georgina and Harriet into the bungalow.

Harriet went and put the kettle on, while Georgina sat Janie down in her lounge.

Janie wiped her face with the tissues that Georgina gave her.

'I am sorry Mrs Wright, I will be alright now, it was just an argument with my mum.'

Harriet brought a cup of tea in for Janie, who seemed a lot calmer now.

Georgina didn't want to push Janie for information. She looked very pale with dark shadows under her eyes.

'I didn't know you were back home Janie. Your mother told us you had gone away to college up north somewhere,' Harriet said.

'Yes, I have been away, but came home this evening.'

At that moment, there was a loud knocking on Georgina's front door and the bell was being pushed as well.

As Georgina opened the door, Mrs Roberts, Janie's mother pushed her to one side and rushed into the lounge.

'Old Bob from the cottages told me he saw my Jane come in to your house,' she said to Georgie and turned to Janie. 'Come along home now Janie, this minute.'

Turning to Harriet and Georgina, Mrs Roberts glared at them and said. 'Whatever she has told you it's all lies, she fantasises. We just had an argument over her clothes. Now come on Janie, thank Mrs Wright for the tea we are going home.'

Janie glared at her mother, smiled weakly at Harriet and Georgina and replaced her cup onto the coffee table and walked reluctantly out the front door followed by her mother.

'Just a family disagreement,' Mrs Roberts said, as she went out slamming the door behind her.

'Whatever that was about, Janice Roberts didn't want us to know, in fact she seemed scared that Janie had told us something she wanted kept secret!'

'Yes, very weird,' Harriet said, 'More to this than meets the eye.'

The Truth

Saturday Morning

The next day after the altercation with Mrs Roberts, Georgina was pulling a few weeds out of her front garden, when she became aware that Janie was hovering outside her front gate.

'Hello Janie,' Georgina got up off her knees and went to the front gate. 'Would you like a cup of tea?'

Janie hesitated then nodded her head.

'Your mother isn't going to come and shout at me again, I hope.'

'No, mother has gone to Palmouth,' Janie said.

They both went into Georgina's bungalow and she put the kettle on.

'Are you alright now love? If you would like a chat, but if not, we will just have a cup of tea and piece of the cherry cake I made this morning.' Georgina felt the girl was still troubled, but didn't want to pressurise her.

'I am sorry my mum went off on one last night. She doesn't understand.' Janie's eyes filled with tears.

Georgina went and sat on the sofa next to Janie.

'If I can help, even by just listening to whatever is worrying you.' Georgina took the girl's hand.

Janie hesitated then she started to talk.

~~Georgina went and sat on the sofa next to Janie.~~

The story that Georgina was told, was a very sad story and it twanged Georgina's heart strings, in fact, by the end of the conversation Georgina felt near to tears herself.

Janie finished her tea and piece of cake and thanked Georgina for listening. Georgina promised to try and think of a way to help the girl, but it did seem an unsolvable problem.

After Janie had left her, Georgina sat and tried to think of a way to help the girl and especially how to do it without upsetting her family.

Her thoughts went round and round but no solution presented itself. She decided she needed the advice of her free-thinking friend Harriet. She got her coat and trotted over to Harriet's house.

'Hello Georgie. I thought you were having a go in your garden today!' Harriet said, when Georgina opened her kitchen door and popped her head inside.

'I was doing some weeding. Young Janie came along the lane and I could see she was deliberating whether or not to come in and see me, so I invited her in for a cup of tea.'

'Did she tell you what the drama was all about?' Harriet put the kettle on and got two mugs out.

She could see that something was bothering Georgina.

'The story is so sad, it really upset me!'

With the coffee made, both the women took their cups into Harriet's lounge, and settled down for what was going to be a long disturbing discussion.

'You know her mother told us that Janie had gone away to some training college up north. That was apparently a blind. Janie was pregnant and her mother arranged for her to go to a mother and baby home up in the north somewhere. You remember when the fair was in Palmouth on the Wellington Green?'

'Yes, it was there for most of last summer,' Harriet said.

'Janie got talking to the lad who parents owned the fair. One thing led to another and they started going out. Her mother didn't know and certainly wouldn't have been very happy about it. Just before the fair was due to leave Palmouth, Janie discovered she was pregnant. The boy, Nelson, all due to him, left his job with the fair and stayed on in Palmouth. He got a job at the packing factory on the Wellington Industrial Estate.

'Once Mrs Roberts found out Janie was pregnant, she went ballistic. The boyfriend came to see Mrs Roberts, but once she found out that he came from a gypsy family from the fair she threw him out and banned Janie from seeing him. She then made arrangements for Janie to go and stay with her aunt up north, until the mother and baby home would take her in.

'Janie tried desperately to change her mother's mind, without success. Janie's step-father and his mates went and found the lad and they gave him a battering. Janie only found that out when she met up with Nelson again.

'Janie had still been secretly meeting her boyfriend and was upset when the lad didn't turn up at their usual meeting place and she thought that he had decided to re-join the fair and abandon her. In fact, he was in hospital from the attack, which Janie knew nothing about. In those couple of weeks Janie was shipped off to her aunt's, feeling very lonely and unhappy.'

Harriet could see that this story had really upset her friend.

'Oh, my goodness, what a sad story!' Harriet said.

'Yes, it gets worse!'

'Janie stayed with her aunt Helen, who apparently was not such a dragon as Janie's mother, until she could go to the Mother and Baby home.

'Her son was born with no problems and was a healthy little lad. She had told Helen that she didn't want to give her child up for adoption. Her aunt took her and her baby boy back to her flat when she left the Home and encouraged her to try and contact Nelson again. Janie phoned Nelson who was delighted to hear from Janie.

'He told Janie that he had gone to see Janie's mother after he got out of the hospital and was told that Janie had lost the baby and didn't want to see him again.'

'Oh, what an awful thing to do,' Georgina said.

'The boy then left his job in Palmarsh and went after his family, back to the fair. He was amazed when Janie told him that he had a son.

'After he received the phone call from Janie, he spoke to his father, who gave him one of his vans and told him to go and find his son. Nelson turned up at Janie's aunts within hours and was in tears when he saw his son.

'Janie had not named her son, hoping to speak to Nelson first. Janie and her aunt had called him 'Little Bear'. So, Nelson and Janie decided his name would be Edward, after Nelson's father and William after Janie's dad, Teddy for short!'

'How sweet,' Harriet said.

'They knew that they couldn't stay with aunt Helen, as she only had a one-bedroom flat. They decided to return south and go and see Janie's mother. Helen had thought that once her sister saw her grandson, she may have a change of heart.

'They left aunt Helen's and drove back to Gorlstone yesterday. Nelson had parked up past your house and Janie took baby Teddy over to see her mother. It was nearly dark, so Janie was able to get to the house without being spotted. She also knew that in all probability Jason, that chap that lives with her mother, would be at the pub. Fortunately, he was.

'But her mother was furious with her for turning up with the child, and they had a row. Janie told me that Nelson had followed her to the house and when he heard Mrs Roberts saying she was going to call the welfare to come and take the child, Nelson went into the house and took the baby and ran off.

'Remember the person who ran past us as we were walking over to get your pattern. That must have been Nelson, and now I think about it, I said he was carrying something. Must have been the baby.'

'So, the screaming we heard was Janie and her mother.'

'Yes, Janie said her mother tried to stop her from following Nelson. But she got away and that was when we saw her in that state. Nelson had driven off, by the time Janie got into Cherry Lane.

'Janie went back home with her mother, and then later crept out and caught the bus Palmarsh. She went to the flat that Nelson had stayed in with his friend Tim, only to find that Nelson had been there with the child but had disappeared. She came back to her mother's, hoping Nelson would be here. But there is no sign of him. Janie is desperate.'

'Poor girl, what can we do?' Harriet was very moved by the story.

'That is still not all. Last night, after Janie caught the bus to Palmarsh, Jason returned from the pub. Janice Roberts told him that Janie had returned.

'He lost his temper and they had an almighty row. Janice let slip that the baby hadn't been adopted and that made things worse. Jason slammed out of the house and Janice thought he had gone back to the pub. But it turns out he got in his truck and drove to Palmouth.

'And now to crown it all, this morning the police have been to tell Janie and Janice that his body was found in Palmouth Park last night. He has been murdered.'

'Oh my God! You don't think he went to find the boy, do you?'

'That's what Janie is worried about,' Georgina said.

Retribution

The Evening Before

Janie had returned to Gorlstone after she had visited Tim in Palmouth, the evening that Nelson had taken their baby. She had tried repeatedly to contact Nelson.

Tim, Nelson's friend was also very concerned, that Nelson had disappeared.

Tim told Janie, that Nelson had arrived at his flat with baby Teddy, but told him he had to buy nappies and milk powder for the baby. He had taken the baby with him and as far as Tim knew, he had gone across the park to the late-night opening chemist's shop in the parade of shops on the other side of the park. That was the last Tim had seen of Nelson.

Janie had wanted to walk across the park to see if she could find him, but Tim had not been happy for her to go across the park, alone, in the dark.

'He might come back the main road way and you would miss him, better to wait here.' After an hour, Janie said she was going out to find Nelson. Tim said he would go with her.

As they crossed the road to enter the park, they became aware of blue flashing lights and police sirens going into the park.

'What is going on, perhaps something has happened to Nelson and Teddy.' Janie was beginning to panic.

'Stay here Janie by the street light, I will run across the cricket pitch where its dark and try and see what's going on. Now promise me you will stay here.'

Janie was very scared, so she stood by the park railings while Tim sprinted across the grass towards the blue lights.

After about five minutes he returned.

'I saw an old boy who was walking his dog. He told me that another dog walker and his Labrador had found a man's body. Its ok, don't panic Janie. The old man told me that it was a fat bald bloke. Apparently, he thinks the man is dead. No sign of a pushchair or Nelson. Let's get back to the flat he may be back there.'

When they had got back to Tim's flat, there was still no sign of Nelson. Tim went round the back of his flat to his parking space and found that Nelson's van was gone as well.

Tim couldn't explain it, unless he had gone back to Gorlstone to find Janie. So, Janie had caught the next bus back to her mother's, hoping that Jason wouldn't be there.

Fortunately, her mother was alone and Janice seemed pleased to see her daughter. The fight she'd had with Jason before he had stormed off, had left her with a bruised arm and a black eye, and a resolve to tell him not to come back, and she was feeling a little guilty about the row she had with Janie.

Without much conversation, Janie ate the meal her mother had prepared and both were happy to get to bed, not that either of them slept very much.

The next morning, Janie woke up at seven. She had got straight up and put her dressing gown on.

When she got downstairs, she found her mother in the kitchen, about to make a cup of tea.

'Still take two sugars love?' her mother asked.

'Yes, please. I know this is not the first time he has hit you.'

Janice coloured up.

'If I stayed, and he hit you or touched Teddy, I would kill him! I hate him!'

'I told him not to come back Janie. I am not going to be his punch bag any longer!'

Janie dialled Nelson's mobile number several times through the night, but only got the message that his phone was switched-off. She sat down and had eaten some toast, and drank her cup of tea.

She tried Nelson's phone again, but still got the unavailable message.

Janie decided she would go into Palmouth again, to see if Nelson had returned to his friend Tim's flat. She was just going up the stairs to get dressed, when a knock came on her mother's front door. Her mother came and opened the front door to find two police officers standing on the doorstep.

Janie came back down the stairs as her mother spoke to the two police officers. 'We have this address for Jason Bishop, does he live here?' The younger officer asked Janice.

'Yes, he does live here. Why do you want him?' Janice asked quietly.

'Can we come in? We need to speak with you.'

They followed Janice back into the kitchen.

Janie followed the officers into her mother's kitchen.

'I am afraid Mr Bishop's body was found in Palmouth Park last night. I am sorry to tell you, but he has been murdered.'

Janice sat down as her legs suddenly went very weak.

'Can you get your mother a cup of tea, love?' The older police officer said to Janie.

Janie was suddenly very frightened. When she returned with the tea for her mother, the police officers were firing questions at her.

'When did you last see Mr Bishop?'

Janice tried very hard to concentrate her thoughts.

'He left here about six last night,' Janice told the officers.

'You seem to have an injury to your face, Mrs Roberts!'

'He hit my mother, he is a bastard,' Janie told the officers.

'We had a difference of opinion, that's all. He had been in the pub. He said what he had to say and then stomped off. This is usual, but this time I told him not to come back, I have had enough of him.'

'What exactly was the row about?' The younger officer asked Janice.

'Janie had been away at college and returned yesterday. Jason had put his fishing gear in her bedroom, I asked him to remove it and he just went off on one!' As Janice spoke, she looked at Janie, hoping to convey the unspoken message to keep her mouth shut.

'Has Mr Bishop got any relations in the area. We would like any addresses you may have for them. Someone will have to come down and formerly identify him. Probably not a job for you, Mrs Roberts.'

'He has a half-brother who lives in Downton, near Salisbury, but they don't have a lot to do with each other. I know Jason went to see him about a month ago, I will get the address for you.'

She found her address book and gave the officers Jason's brother's address.

'He had a skin-full of booze before he left here. He had been in the Plough across the road most of the afternoon, which was not unusual.'

'He was badly beaten up. Can you tell me if Mr Bishop had any enemies?'

Janice shrugged her shoulders, 'I don't know any of his work mates.'

The police officers decided to leave further questioning till later, and told Janice that she would be required to come to the police station to make a formal statement.

'We will send a car for you later today, to bring you to Palmouth.'

With that, the police officers got up and left.

Janie and her mother sat and looked at each other. Neither knowing what to say. Both had fearful thoughts. Janie more than her mother. Where was Nelson and her baby? Had Jason found Nelson?

There was a tap on the back door and Joe Clarke came into the kitchen, where Janice and Janie sat drinking another cup of tea.

'Are you ok Jan? I saw the cop's car outside.'

Joe came in and put his hand on Janie's shoulder.

He was a local farmer and had been a good friend of William, Janice's deceased husband.

'It's Jason, he was found dead last night in Palmouth Park.'

'Bloody hell, Jan. He was a loud-mouthed bastard, and to be honest, in the pub last night we had words. He was bad mouthing Janie and it didn't go down with me and the lads in the pub. He got stroppy. Are you ok Janie?' Joe asked Janie. She nodded as she poured out a cup of tea for Joe.

Janie had always like him and had hoped that her mother would take up with Joe, after her dad died, but Jason had muscled in and her mother had not given Joe a second look.

'I am sorry to speak ill of the dead Jan, but Jason was not a nice person. There will be quite a few people relieved that he will not be causing anymore grief.' Joe took Janice's hand. 'If there is anything I can do, you know where am, and that applies to you both.'

Joe got up to go, and Janice stood up and went to the back door with him.

'Thank you, Joe, please call in again, it is a comfort.'

Janice came back into the kitchen and suddenly she was very pleased that Janie was with her.

'I am sorry love for the way I have carried on about the baby. Jason was a bully and sometimes terrified me. I knew he would never allow you to bring the baby or Nelson to the house. I sometimes thought, I had made a mistake having him here, but once you do these things it's hard to reverse things and I was lonely.

'Jason did have a lot of enemies and he was capable of bad things, I am sure. All I hope is that he didn't run into your gypsy lad.'

'Oh, mum that's what worries me. You don't think that was what happened do you?'

'We say nothing about any of that. You must try and find Nelson and the baby and keep them well away until this is sorted out,' Janice told her daughter.

Both women were afraid to think too much.

Later that morning, a patrol car came and took Janice into Palmouth to make her statement. She told Janie that she would do her Tesco shopping while she was there and would return on the bus.

Janie so badly wanted someone to talk to someone. She had decided to go and see Mrs Wright, while her mother was in town and was pleased to see her in her front garden, and hadn't hesitated when Georgina invited her in.

Later that day, the two women were sitting in Harriet's kitchen, discussing the conversation Georgina had with Janie that morning.

They had heard on the morning news, the account of Jason's body being found in the park the evening before.

'I wish we could sort little Janie's problem out for her. I just don't know how to help her.' Georgina poured more coffee into both their cups and the two women sat pondering.

'I saw a police car outside her mother's house earlier. I think Janice went off with the police. She had to make a statement I suppose. I just hope they don't ask her to identify that awful man's body.'

Harriet had watched from the old bakery window when she had gone in, to see if any letters for the owner had been delivered.

Now Georgina understood, how Janie had been able to come over to see her that morning and tell her story, without her mother chasing after her.

'How about us going into Palmouth, and having a late some lunch in the Park Hotel. They serve food all day there. We might pick up some information.'

'Oh Harry, are you in Sherlock mode again?'

'Well, it wouldn't hurt to have a poke around! That poor girl is desperate. Fortunately, her mother seems to be more supportive—too late of course.'

'Ok, shall we drive in or get the bus?' Georgina asked.

'Think we will go on the bus, then we could have a glass of wine if we decide to have lunch.'

They both had been thinking about Nelson and the baby. The police had not released any more details apart from Jason's name. They had asked for any witnesses who had been in the park on Friday evening to come forward.

The two ladies caught the next bus into ~~Palmarsh~~. They went to the bus station and decided to walk back through the park to the Park Hotel. About halfway across, they could see blue and white tapes fluttering around an area in a corner under the trees a few yards from the pathway.

'That must be where they found the body. What's that laying by the tree? Looks like a bunch of flowers.'

Georgina bent down under the police tapes and ran over to the tree. She stooped down to look at the small label attached to the flowers.

Harriet stayed on the path.

'What you doing Georgie? Who would leave flowers for that tow rag?'

Georgina came back to the path and got out her pen and notebook and scribbled something.

'No don't think they are from Janice; I will show you when we get to the pub. Let's not hang around here, people will think we are vultures.'

When the ladies got to the Park Hotel, they were able to find a table. The pub was still quite busy even though it was nearing three.

They looked at the menu and decided to order some food. Georgina ordered a pasta bake and Harriet, a steak and kidney pie.

Harriet suddenly said, 'Isn't that Janie over there talking to that fair haired young man?'

Georgina nodded. She got her notebook out of her bag.

'This is what was written on the card, left with that bunch of flowers.'

Harriet took the notebook.

'You wanted us to dance, now we will dance on your grave.'

'My God someone didn't like him.' Harriet said.

'I should have taken a photo on my phone, they were marigolds, but wrapped round them was deadly nightshade.'

'Crikey, do you think the police have seen it?'

At that moment, Janie came over to their table accompanied by the fair-haired young chap she had been talking to. Both women changed the subject and Georgina hurriedly put her notebook away.

Saturday Afternoon

'Hello Mrs Wright and Mrs Holt, this is Tim, Nelson's friend.'

Harriet pulled up two chairs from an adjoining table and indicated that the young couple join them.

'Have you eaten Janie? If not, let us treat you to a nice lunch.'

Janie looked so pale and Harriet knew she didn't have much money and guessed she hadn't eaten.

She gave a menu to Janie and the boy.

'Thank you, Mrs Holt.'

'Now I think it's time that you call us Harriet and Georgina,' Georgina said, as she beckoned the waitress over to take their order. 'Have whatever you like.'

While they were waiting for their food, Harriet gently asked Janie how things were going and asked if she had heard from Nelson.

Janie seemed relieved to be able to talk about the events of the previous two days.

Janie and Tim told Harriet and Georgina what had happened, when she had come to Palmouth looking for Nelson on Friday evening.

A tear ran down Janie's face, Harriet passed her a tissue.

'I was terrified it was Nelson, but the man Tim spoke to, said it was a fat bald man,' Janie said tearfully.

'We thought he might have come back to Tim's, but his van was gone!'

'What has happened to him? I am afraid that he met Jason and…'

'No, Janie don't even go there, we don't know. All I know is that he will be taking great care of your son.'

Harriet put her arms around Janie.

'Let's eat our lunch. You have to keep strong. I suggest you keep Nelson out of things, at the moment.'

While they were waiting for their food, Harriet noticed someone she recognised. It was one of the police officers she had seen going into Janice and Janie's house. He was talking to the bar maid and the landlord. The bar maid then followed the police officer through to the Snug Bar.

As Harriet was the only one sitting facing the bar, neither Janie or Tom had seen the police officer speaking to the bar maid. She excused herself from the table to 'powder her nose', and made her way to the passage that passed by the Snug. She stooped to untie her laces on her shoe, at the slightly open doorway. She could hear the conversation very clearly. She hovered as long as she could, and as the bar maid and the officer left the Snug, they nearly fell over Harriet who was bending down struggling with a knotted shoe lace.

Harriet returned to their table after a brief conversation.

The meals were brought to the table and although Janie didn't think she would be able to eat, surprisingly, she enjoyed her lunch and felt a lot better after.

'Have you told the police anything about Nelson and Teddy?' Georgina asked.

'No, my mum said to say nothing. No-one in the village saw Nelson or Teddy, I don't think'

'Have you tried phoning him?'

'His phone is switched off,' Tim said. 'I told Janie not to use her to phone, in case the police want to check her phone. If they get a whisper about Nelson, they will go looking for him.'

As they sat at their table after they had eaten, Janie said that she would return to Gorlstone on the bus with Harriet and Georgina.

'I will stay with my mum. Jason was a bully, and she had told him not to come back. He gave her a black eye and bruised her arm before he left. Hopefully, Nelson will phone me. I don't know what else to do.'

'Do you think Nelson has gone back to his family with Teddy?' Harriet asked.

'Let's catch the bus back home, we can discuss what to do next when we get home,' Georgina said as they left their table. They said goodbye to Tim, and the three of them walked to the bus stop.

Flight

Friday Evening

Nelson drove north as fast as was safe and legal. Teddy was sleeping in a large heavy duty cardboard box that Nelson had found folded up in the back of his father's van. Nelson intended to buy a baby car seat at the first opportunity, but to be away from the area was more important.

The pushchair was folded up in the back of the van. There was blood on one of the wheels. Nelson had thought of abandoning the pushchair in Palmouth, but then realised Janie's finger prints were probably on the handles as were his own, so he couldn't risk leaving it anywhere the police could, would find it, and so incriminate Janie.

He knew that once he got back to his family, they would protect him and Teddy. It was the Romany way.

The family would close ranks.

Palmarsh Police Station

Saturday Morning

Jason's brother Mark, had driven from Downton, to formerly identify his brother on Saturday morning. He wasn't greatly surprised when the police called at his home earlier that morning, and told him that Jason had been attacked. He knew that his brother had mixed with some rum characters over years. Several years ago, Jason had spent a few months at her Majesties pleasure, for receiving stolen goods. Mark knew Jason had got off lightly, as he had been convinced at the time, that Jason had actually been the brains behind the raid that had broken into a warehouse.

The actual identification hadn't been so easy as he had thought. Seeing his brother laying in the mortuary was traumatic and after he had identified the body, he was very glad to be driving back to his home.

Detective Inspector, Paul Kennedy had been put in charge of the murder case. Paul was forty-eight years old and had risen through the ranks fairly quickly. He had a history of being an astute judge of character and his success rate was unquestionable. Because of his dedication to his job, his marriage had failed four years ago. His wife got tired of the long hours her husband spent at the police station and had moved out and had married a stock broker, very quickly, after the divorce. She now had a lifestyle far above that which a police officer could have offered her.

His Sergeant, Clive Robbins had worked intensively with Inspector Kennedy on many previous cases.

Clive was thirty-two years old and was unmarried. Both officers had attended the scene of crime on the previous evening, when the body had been found.

'The old boy who found the body has been interviewed, but I want WPC Jones to go and see the old chap this afternoon. He was a bit shook up, so he may now remember something he forgot at the time.'

Inspector Kennedy had set up a board with the crime scene photos on.

'I am going over to see the woman he lived with, and her daughter. I am not convinced she told us everything in her statement. You come with me Clive, I want you to go over to the pub and talk to the landlord.'

The Inspector and Sergeant Robbins left the police station. Leaving instructions for his officers to do a door-to-door search of the area around the park. The park had already been searched first thing that morning.

On arriving at Gorlstone, Inspector Kennedy went straight to Janice's house.

Janice was expecting a visit. She had been taken to the police station earlier to make a statement and had returned on the bus, after doing some shopping. Janie had caught the bus to Palmouth after she had spoken to Georgina as she wanted to go and see Nelson's friend Tim again.

They had both agreed to say nothing about Nelson and Teddy.

'Good afternoon, Mrs Roberts. I am sorry to worry you, but there are a few more questions I would like to clarify with you.'

Janice took the Inspector into her kitchen.

'Now Mrs Roberts, how long was Jason living here with you?'

'He stayed here most nights lately. Before that, it was just weekends. I suppose it's the last six months that he started to stay over-night,' Janice told the Inspector.

'Do you know where he stayed when he wasn't with you?'

This had been a question that Janice had asked Jason several times, but had been answered with a, 'what's it got to do with you' comment. Janice had never pushed for an answer, she got the impression that she would rather not know!

'I don't really know. I think he may have stayed over with his drinking mates; he did like a drink.'

The Inspector, having spoken to the doctor performing the post-mortem and had been made aware, that Jason was smelling strongly of alcohol when taken to the mortuary.

'Where did Jason mainly drink?'

'Most afternoons, lately, he would be over the road in the Plough from about four. He would come home for his dinner, then either sit and go to sleep till bedtime or he would go back over the Plough.'

'I thought Jason worked on a building site in Palmouth?'

'Yes, he does, I mean he did, but always got back here to the village by four each day.'

'Did Jason's post come here?'

Janice shook her head. No letters had ever come to her house for Jason. She knew that Jason was not very literate, and although he read the racing paper, she had never seen him write a letter. She hadn't even thought about it until the Inspector mentioned it.

There were a few more questions which Janice couldn't answer. It occurred to her after that there was quite a lot that she didn't know about the man that she had let into her life.

When she was asked about Janie, she told the police officer that Janie had gone to see a friend in Palmouth. She told him that Janie had got on alright with Jason to a degree, but didn't have a lot to do with him. She had been very attached to her father, so wasn't going to go overboard on another man in his place.

Inspector Kennedy left Janice's house, not having learned a lot more than before. He told Janice that he would like to talk to Janie again within the next few days. He had formed the idea that the daughter didn't like Jason.

Sergeant Robbins, on the other hand, was hearing a lot about the victim from the drinkers in the Plough Inn. None of what he was hearing was very complimentary.

He introduced himself to Tom, the landlord and listened quietly when he was given chapter and verse regarding the many incidents of Jason's bad behaviour.

Tom confirmed that Jason had come into the Plough at about three-thirty on Friday afternoon.

'He was his usual chopsy self. He just couldn't keep his mouth shut. In the end, I had to chuck him out.'

'Who did he upset then?'

'Me, for a start. He had words with Joe Clarke and the boys who are working on the barn conversion up the street. Mick, Scott and Jack. He was a nasty piece of work. My missus wasn't too happy with him either.'

'I will need to speak to these lads as well. But can you tell me what was said?' Clive got his notebook out and wrote down the names of the customers who were in the pub the evening before.

'He was running Janie down; you know Mrs Robert's daughter. Calling her a slag and one of Scott's daughters as well. I've known Janice and Janie, since Janie was a little girl. It hasn't been easy for Janie's since her dad died. Janice has done her best, she does a few shifts here for me in the kitchen if I am busy. Janie is a nice kid.

'Then he had a go at me, implying that my wife has had an affair, not true by the way. My wife heard him and I could have killed him! Oops, suppose I shouldn't say that under the circumstances.'

The Sergeant made a note in his book, 'check out landlord's wife'.

'Where do these other chaps live? In the village?'

'Joe Clarke lives along Cherry Lane; he has the first farm. The other three live in Palmouth, they are working up the road as I said, just up the hill. I doubt they will be there today; they don't usually work on a Saturday.'

'I will drive up and have a look at the site before I go back to the station.'

Clive was just putting his notebook back into his pocket when the pub door opened.

'Hello Joe, this copper was just asking about Friday afternoon when I had to throw Jason out.'

'Huh, that bastard. Not surprising someone topped him. Sorry mate,' Joe said turning to the Sergeant. 'What Jan saw in him; I do not know!'

'Can you give me your version of events, when Jason was here in the pub? Also, after you left the pub where did you go Mr Clarke?'

Joe told the Sergeant all that he could remember. He also admitted that he was very fond of both Janice and Janie.

'Jan's husband was one of my best friends. It was so sad that he died. I promised him that I would always look out for Jan and Janie. Once that fat bastard got his foot in her door, she seemed to change. I think in a way she was afraid of him.'

'You were not happy about Mrs Robert's relationship with Jason Bishop then? After you left the Plough on Friday afternoon, where did you go Mr Clarke?'

'I went back to the farm. I had to feed my cattle and chickens. Then I had a bath and then worked on my farm accounts till I went to bed,' Joe said. 'Yes, I hated Jason. Will, Jan's husband, also disliked him. He has form, he has been in prison. I don't know if Jan knows, wasn't my place to tell her, but I just kept an eye on him.'

'Is there anyone who can confirm that you were at home all the evening?'

'No, I live alone.'

Tom, the landlord interrupted, 'Joe is a good man, he has no reason to lie. He has always looked out for Jan and Janie. Why she had to let that wanker Jason move in with her, I don't know.'

The Sergeant told them that he would probably have more questions, but for now he was going to drive up to the building site, to see if there was anyone about.

Clive decided to walk the 200 yards up the main street to the site, where the men who had been in the pub on Friday afternoon, worked. The site was closed off with a large steel gate. He noticed a board giving the details of the builder carrying out the renovations. The Sergeant took details of the company's telephone number and office address and then made his way back to the squad car. The Inspector soon joined him and they drove back to the station.

'The farmer who had words with Bishop in the Plough, obviously has the hots for Mrs Roberts, but he says he left the pub and went straight home.' Clive told his boss. 'The landlord said that the builders who were in the pub also had words with Bishop. As a result, Bishop was told to leave the pub!'

'Gives them all motives to have a go at Bishop, and without anyone to substantiate the farmer was at home all evening, we won't write him off.' The Inspector was very thoughtful on the way back to Palmouth.

When they arrived, there were several reports laying on the Inspector's desk, from the house-to-house visits by beat officers.

'Get me some coffee and come and join me, we will go through these. Also round up the officers who did the footwork on these reports, if they are still on duty. It will be quicker than trawling through every one of these.'

Constables, Alice Woodrow and Derek Baines followed Sergeant Robbins into Paul Kennedy's office, when he came back with the coffee.

'Only these two still here guv, the others were on the early shift and have signed off.'

'Ok, anything come to light, anyone see anything?'

The Inspector sat down behind his desk and invited the officers to sit.

'I started on the far side of the park. I went into the shops to see if anyone had seen Bishop. He had a new packet of cigarettes in his pocket when he was found, I thought he might have bought them down in the newsagents.'

'Good thinking Derek, there was also a copy of the evening paper found near his body.'

'The old boy in the newsagents knew Bishop. He said he was an ignorant prat; he never ever said please or thank you, and was usually smelling of booze. Apparently, he did go in last night to buy fags and an evening paper. He said after he left his shop, he heard Bishop shouting abuse at someone outside. He couldn't see who he was shouting at, as he was serving another customer.'

'Well at least we know he went down to the shops last night. Did you go into any of the other shops?' Paul Kennedy asked.

'I went into the chemists next door and the girl in there, a dopey blonde bit, said she was serving a man with a baby in a pushchair. As this chap went out of the shop, she saw a bald bloke waving his arms about and seemed to be shouting at this man.'

The Inspector sat up in his chair, 'Is there CCTV along the front of those shops?'

'I don't know, I didn't think to ask,' Derek said.

'What happened after Bishop was shouting?'

Constable Baines was feeling uncomfortable, as he hadn't thought to ask about the CCTV.

'The girl said, she thought that the bloke with the pushchair went off up the street but couldn't remember which way he went. I'll get onto the shops straight away and see if there is any CCTV footage.'

'WPC Woodrow what have you got to put in the pot?' Kennedy asked.

Alice always felt very self-conscious around Paul Kennedy. Truth be told, she had dreams of him at night in romantic situations, but this was something she wouldn't want anyone to know about.

'I started at the top of the park. No-one in the houses opposite the park entrance, heard anything until the sirens started when the ambulance arrived. I did go into the Park Hotel and spoke to the bar staff there. The bar maid told me that some workmen came in the early evening, and she did hear them mention Jason Bishop's name. She said they sounded 'pissed off', if you'll excuse the swearing, but that is what she said. I tried to get her to say more, but she clammed up. I got her name, Sheryl Davies.'

'Clive get yourself over to the Park Hotel later, and put your undoubted charms onto Miss Davies, and find out who the workmen were that were mouthing off about Bishop, and you, Constable Baines go down and sort out the CCTV query, and bring back any film for the last forty-eight hours, if it exists.'

'Yes guv.' Derek left the Inspector's office like a scalded cat!

Kennedy turned to Alice, 'Type up your interview now, the one you had with the bar maid, and make sure Clive gets it before he goes to see the bar maid later, and the notes on the houses you checked on. Then I want you to look up Jason

Bishop, as the Sergeant seems to think he may have some previous run-ins with the law.'

Later that day, after Sergeant Robbins had typed up his reports from the interviews at Gorlstone. He had a call from the laboratory that needed his attention. Constable Baines phoned to say he was having problems obtaining the CCTV film from the parade of shops.

So, the Sergeant took a car down to the shops and found constable Baines.

'What's the problem Derek?'

'The manager of the chemists has gone to his sisters in Bath for the day, and the woman in charge in the newsagents doesn't know how to take the film out and refuses to let me do it, and to be honest, I don't know how to do it either. I am afraid I could delete it all!'

'Oh, that would not please the guvnor, let me talk to the woman.'

After a heated discussion, Clive persuaded the newsagent's manager to allow him access to the CCTV camera. It was soon obvious that it would be afternoon, before Clive got over to the Park Hotel.

He combed his hair before he got out of his car. He had floppy blonde hair that was always falling across his face. He always looked as though he needed a shave, but the designer stubble seemed to attract the ladies. The only trouble was, as Romeo's go, although Clive had the looks, he hadn't got a clue on the finesse required to chat up a woman, and often ended up with the female in question running for the hills.

He went to the bar and ordered a glass of orange juice and as he was given his change, he asked the boy serving the drinks, if Sheryl was working tonight. He was told that Sheryl was due to start five minutes ago, she was late as usual he was told.

The pub smelled of the meals that some customers were consuming. It made Clive feel hungry. Both he and the Inspector had been up most of the night while the 'Scene of Crime' officers had been searching the murder scene.

A table to one side, had three old gents sitting playing crib. He also noticed Janie Roberts and a young man sitting at a table by the window with two old ladies, obviously having had their lunch there. One of the old ladies, watched Clive as he was speaking to the lad behind the bar. 'Probably her granny.' Clive thought.

Clive took his drink to a table near to the bar, intending to wait to speak to the bar maid.

He didn't have long to wait. He heard loud words being said in the room behind the bar, then a rather dishevelled female pranced into the bar.

Clive walked over and showed Sheryl his warrant card. 'Can I have a word, Miss Davies?'

'What's this all about? I got to work, and I just got a bollicking from the boss cos I was a few minutes late.'

Felix the landlord, who Clive knew very well, was standing in the doorway to the cellar. Clive beckoned to him, 'Look Felix, we are investigating the death of one of your customers. It is important that I speak to all your staff who were on duty on Friday night. I'd like to speak to Miss Davies, I can take her and other members of your staff to the station right now, but if you will let me speak to them in your Snug, then I won't have to disrupt your staff. I won't keep them long.'

Felix nodded, seeing the sense in the Sergeant's request. At the moment, the pub was not too busy but later he would need all his staff on duty.

Sheryl Davies followed Sergeant Robbins into the small Snug Bar at the rear of the pub.

'Now Sheryl, I believe you spoke to Jason Bishop last night. What time did he come into the pub?'

Sheryl had to think.

'I started work at four and it must have been about five-thirty, no, just a minute, it was later. I had been watching the tv and when the news came on, that was when I went back into the bar. Jason came in soon after that. He had a pint, although, I could tell it wasn't his first that day. He went to the fag machine and then came back and had a go at me, cos the brand of ciggy's that he smokes had run out. The bloke who fills the fag machine only comes on Monday. Jason finished his pint then stormed out of the pub, swearing like a trooper.'

'You think he was going to the shop to get his cigarettes?' Clive asked.

'Yes, think that's what he was saying as he went out.'

'Did you see Bishop again Friday on night?'

'No, the next I heard was the police sirens but we didn't know what was happening.'

Sheryl seemed a little upset and Clive thought he would push her a bit more.

'Did you know Jason Bishop other than as a customer in here? You are a local girl and Bishop was also a local.'

Sharon looked decidedly uncomfortable.

'We went to the same school and I have been out with him once, but I am engaged to be married to Ronnie Porter, and he mustn't know. You won't tell him will you?'

Clive wrote down Sheryl's fiancé's name in his notebook.

'When was the last time you saw Jason, apart from here in the pub?'

'He called round to me mum's a week or so ago, he knows me mum goes to Bingo on a Friday night.'

Clive wrote this down in his notebook, he said nothing, hoping Sheryl would continue talking, 'I let him in, as I didn't want our nosy neighbour to see him on the doorstep. He told me he wanted me to go out with him again.'

'So, you had been in a relationship with Jason before, as you only said you had been out with him once before.'

Sheryl blushed and looked even more uncomfortable.

'Well, we did have a bit of a fling, but he was so domineering and when he was drunk once, he hit me, so I stopped seeing him. My step-dad had words with him and told him to keep away.'

'What is your step-father's name Sheryl? I may have to speak with him.'

'My step-father is dead, so he can't help you and he couldn't have killed Jason, if that's what you think!'

'Did you leave the pub at any time on Friday evening, after Jason walked out?' Clive asked as he put his notebook away.

'No, I didn't even have a tea break, as Felix went off somewhere and it got busy.'

Clive got up and Sheryl left the snug, bumping into one of the old ladies who appeared to be fiddling with her shoe laces outside the snug door.

'I am so sorry, but I my shoe laces have come undone and now are knotted. I left my spectacles at my table and I can't see without them,' the elderly lady said.

Clive bent down and untangled the old ladies lace for her.

'Oh, thank you so much,' she said, standing upright.

Flowers, What Flowers?

'You are that young policeman who took my neighbour Janice into Palmouth. I am Harriet Holt, a friend of Janice, I live in Gorlstone. What did you make of the flowers left at the murder scene?' Harriet babbled on.

Clive was edging away from the old woman, then her last comment registered!

'Flowers? We haven't found any flowers.'

'My friend and I saw a bunch by the tree, just before we came in for our lunch.'

Clive thought, 'she's barmy, but I will go and check it out!'

Harriet went back into the bar, and joined her friend Georgina, Janie and Tim.

The young couple thanked Harriet and Georgina for buying their dinner and told them they were going back to Tim's flat and would try again to contact Nelson.

'The officer says they didn't find any flowers at the crime scene.'

Harriet told Georgina after the young couple had left the hotel.

'They were there earlier before we came in here today. Perhaps someone had only just put them there.'

Clive had made a hasty retreat and walked over to the park to look for bunch of flowers.

He walked across the road to the park, when he got to the blue and white tapes that still decorated the scene of the crime, he looked around the tree but could see nothing.

'Silly old bat,' he thought, 'probably talks to herself and sees ghosts!'

Clive went back to police station and wrote up a report of his conversation with Sheryl.

He left a message with the desk Sergeant, for the constables to phone him if there were any developments and got in his car and drove back to his bachelor flat in Palmouth.

Harriet and Georgina caught the bus back to Gorlston. Harriet said nothing on the bus about the conversation she had overheard between the police officer and the bar maid.

Harriet and Georgina went to the Bakery Cottage, Harriet's home, for a cup of tea.

Georgina had been aware that Harriet had been hovering outside the Snug, while the detective was interviewing Sheryl.

Janie and Tom had sat with their backs to the entrance to the Snug, so when Harriet had excused herself to 'spend a penny', they had not realised the real motive behind her penny spending expedition!

'Well, what did you hear, you old snoop!' Georgie asked, as Harriet was making the tea.

'Apparently, Jason had been out with Sheryl about six months ago. He went round to see her again just a week or so ago, while her mother was at Bingo on a Friday night.'

'Do we know her mother? We go most Friday nights, but don't know who Sheryl's mother is?'

Harriet shook her head. 'We could ask that Margaret Sharples, her with the rollers, she knows everyone.'

'I heard her say that her father warned Jason off, as he had hit her when he was drunk. He was told to keep away and Sheryl stopped seeing him. But he came round again last week.'

'I then asked the detective what they made of the bunch of flowers left at the murder scene. He looked at me as though I was daft!'

Georgina rummaged in her bag and found the note she had copied from the note left with the flowers.

'So, you are saying that the police haven't found any flowers? Someone must have put them there today. They couldn't have been there early today, as the police were still sniffing about. We must have been in the park just after the flowers were put there.'

Harriet was trying to think who they had seen in the park, but her mind was blank.

Georgina was thinking.

'I don't think the Sergeant even believed me when I mentioned the bunch of flowers. He looked at me as though I was some silly old fool!' Harriet laughed, as she spoke.

'Think we should ask around, as we promised Janie that we would try and help. If the police find out about Nelson, they will have a ready-made suspect. Why don't we get Tim to chat up Sheryl and try and find out more about Jason.' Georgina thought that.

'We can find out who Sheryl's mother is, at Bingo next Friday. She might tell us how long Sheryl was seeing Jason. He may have been seeing her at the same time he was with Janice.'

Harriet suddenly thought to herself that if that was the case, then it would give Janice a motive to want Jason hurt.

'The trouble is, we might find out something we don't want to. What if Nelson did bash Jason over the head, then buzzed-off with the baby.' Harriet felt awful saying it, but she knew it was a possibility.

The two women got out a pen and paper, and wrote down several scenarios plus the names of the possible suspects.

'I suppose it won't hurt to make some enquiries. The policeman said they had not found any flowers.'

'What did the 'dancing' thing mean on the note? It could be a clue to whoever put the flowers at the scene of crime. But if the police don't believe us about the flowers, then perhaps, we should ask a few questions,' Georgina said thoughtfully.

'Ok, but I am not going to jump out of anymore windows. I have a bruise, the size of a melon, on my bum from the last time we played detective,' Harriet said laughing.

Georgina laughed, and got out her notebook and started a list of possible scenarios;

1. Jason followed Nelson to the park after meeting him outside chemists?
2. Sheryl or family had something to do with Jason's death.
3. Janice found out he was playing away?
4. Janie?
5. Tim?
6. The flowers who put them there and what did the dancing message mean?

'Why have you put Janie and Tim on the list?' Harriet asked.

'We have to be unbiased. We know Janie was in Palmouth and was with Tim. We only have their word that they hadn't gone to find Nelson. They could have met Jason on his way back from the chemist's. We know Jason had bad mouthed Janie at the pub, plus he had been drinking, so they could have met him and had an argument which got out of hand.'

Harriet nodded, it was possible, as much as she hated the idea of suspecting Janie.

'The flowers bother me. What did the note mean?'

'If the police didn't find the flowers, then they couldn't have been there when they found the body, and why has someone now taken them away, unless your policeman friend has removed them. They didn't believe you when you told them, so we can try and follow that up.'

'Tomorrow we will go and see Janice to give her our condolences, and see what she has to say. Perhaps we will have lunch in the Plough. Janie said that Jason was in there before he went to Palmouth.'

Georgina always dressed smartly, and although an inch or two shorter than Harriet, always looked more together than Harriet. She had her hair trimmed and set every fortnight. Harriet washed her own hair and couldn't be bothered with hairdressers.

Harriet had an eclectic view to fashion. Had no idea about designer labels. If she liked the colour of a blouse, it didn't bother her if it went with the rest of her wardrobe. Amazingly, she seemed to get away with her selection of daily apparel.

Georgina often wore skirts. Harriet always favoured trousers, from jeans to baggy concoctions. Her doctrine was, 'if it's comfortable, its ok!'

Both ladies were grey, tinted blond, although Harriet was actually white, but insisted her hair colour was platinum and shoulder length and often straggly, whereas Georgina's hair was always tidy and shorter.

Georgina was petite, while Harriet was what she called podgy!

In actual fact, she did carry a stone or so more than Georgina, but because her clothes were always 'flowing' as she called it, she got away with it.

Their homes were equally different. Harriet's rooms were a collection of the various things she had found impossible to live without. A large table full of Honiton pottery, shelves filled with colourful Poole Pottery and Torquay motto ware. Pictures on the wall were, either ones that Harriet had found in boot fairs or some were her own paintings.

Although seemingly cluttered, her home had a cosy homely feel.

Georgina's according to Harriet, was like a doctor's waiting room. Everything was tidy with a few nice pieces of pottery. The suite, curtains and carpet all cleverly colour matched and spotless.

Georgina, strange as it might seem, actually loved being in Harriet's jumble, as she called it. The two women accepted they were different and quite enjoyed pulling each other's leg.

Without actually discussing the situation, it appeared that they were back on the trail of the facts concerning the events of the past few days.

The two women finished their tea and decided to delve further the following day, starting with Janice and then go to the Plough for a Sunday lunch.

Sunday

Harriet woke up the next day with a thumping headache. She had found it difficult to drop off to sleep the evening before. All the events of the previous days kept rushing round her brain.

She struggled out of bed and put on her dressing gown and went down the stairs.

Her dogs were all eager to get out into the garden. She stood at the back door hoping that the fresh morning air would revive her.

When the dogs had stopped chasing each other, they dashed inside eager for their breakfast. Harriet put the kettle on for her morning cup of tea.

While she was waiting for the kettle to boil, she found the list Georgina had started the evening before.

Who hated Jason? She couldn't actually think of anyone who liked him.

Why would someone want him dead or was it an argument that got out of hand?

If he was seeing Sheryl, was it while he was staying with Janice?

Harriet put her pen down and made the tea and took a couple of paracetamols.

She began to feel a little better. She went back upstairs and got dressed.

The dogs needed their morning walk and their food.

After walking the dogs and they were fed, Harriet put her coat on, locked her doors and went across the road to Georgina's house.

Georgina was also suffering from a disturbed night. Her thoughts galloping around her head all through the night. She had kept wondering where Nelson was and hoped the baby was safe.

She saw Harriet coming up her front path and switched her kettle back on.

The two women sat in Georgina's kitchen, trying to make some sense out of the situation.

The front door bell rang, Georgina looked through the window to see who was on the doorstep.

'It's Joe Clarke, wonder what he wants?' Georgina went to the front door and invited Joe inside.

'I am sorry to bother you, Mrs Wright, but I need some advice.' Joe followed Georgina into her kitchen. 'I'll make you a cup of coffee, looks like you need it.'

Joe sat down and seemed undecided whether he should be there.   coffec

'How can we help you Joe?' Harriet said as Georgina brought in the ~~tea~~ for Joe.

'Last Saturday when I left the pub I told the police that I went straight home and didn't go out again. I had argued with Jason in the pub and I was furious with him.'

Joe looked down at the floor, looking like a guilty school boy.

'So what actually did you do?' Harriet asked, as she passed Joe a cup of coffee.

'I went home, shut the hens up, and then I realised I hadn't anything in for dinner, so I went down to Palmouth to the chippy for fish and chips.'

'As I passed the cottages on the left, about a mile from Gorlstone, I saw Jason's truck parked outside. I carried on to the chippy. As I came out the chip shop when I had bought my supper, Jason's truck tore past. But I did come straight back home then, but I did lie to the police.'

'Well, you could tell them you forgot about getting your supper, the fish shop will confirm that you came in, but of course, they won't know for sure that you went straight back home,' Georgina said.

'I would say nothing at the moment Joe. If they come and see you again, you could then tell them. But if no-one saw you, apart from the fish shop, then I shouldn't worry. You didn't kill Jason did you Joe?'

'Harriet what a thing to say,' Georgina said indignantly.

'No, Mrs Holt, I didn't.'

'Who lives in the cottage where you saw Jason's vehicle parked, as you went to the chippy?' Harriet asked.

'Mandy Streatham, and her daughters.'

Georgina looked at Harriet and said, 'Perhaps she is one of his conquests.'

Joe smiled and handed his empty cup back to Harriet.

'I had better get on, the farrier is coming to trim my donkey's hooves. Thank you for your advice, I feel a lot better for the chat, I will play it by ear. I am sorry for Janice and Janie, but not sorry that Jason is no longer around, he was a bully!'

Georgina showed Joe to the door and came back into her kitchen, very thoughtful.

'Wasn't that Mandy, the one whose husband was found dead in Palmouth?'

Harriet agreed, it had struck her when Joe had mentioned Mandy's name.

The two women then decided to follow their original plan of visiting Janice and then lunch in the Plough.

Janice was not at home when they knocked on her door a little later. It was Janie, who answered the door and invited them in.

'Mother is over at the Plough, helping Tom in the kitchen, as he had a lot of bookings for lunch today,' Janie told them.

'Have you heard anything from Nelson?' Harriet asked.

'Do you promise not to tell my mum or the police?' Janie looked scared.

'No of course we won't tell anyone, but be careful to delete anything on your phone, just in case.' Georgina urged her.

'He phoned me from a call box. The fair is on the move and he stopped in a small village en-route. He just said that Teddy is fine and he will be in touch soon and not to worry. I asked him straight out if he had killed Jason and he was quite upset that I asked. He swore on Teddy's life that he didn't, so I believe him.'

'Well, I believe him, and so do you, don't you Harriet? He wouldn't say that if he was guilty.'

'Do you know Mandy Streatham?' Harriet felt they should know more about this woman.

'I went to school with her eldest daughter Sarah. I think Mrs Streatham's husband died recently. Why do you ask?'

'Oh no reason, her name was mentioned in a conversation I had recently. Well, if you are alright Janie, we will go as we are hoping for a Sunday lunch in the pub and if they are busy, we may be unlucky. Come on Georgina, yorkshire puddings here we come!'

The two women crossed the road to the Plough. Tom greeted them as they entered the bar. They asked him if he had a spare table for them to have lunch. He came from behind the bar and took them to a small table near the window.

'Always got room for you ladies, you will be nice and warm here. You may have a little wait, as there are several in front of you!'

Harriet and Georgina made themselves comfortable.

'Thank you Tom. We are not in a hurry; you just take your time.'

'Think we have to make up our minds where we go from here. We should just let the police get on with it, but if they won't believe that there were flowers laid where they found Jason's body, unless they have taken them, we have a clue they are ignoring!'

Georgina nodded.

'There may be CCTV, at the shops, and if Nelson is on the film someone may recognise him. If they dig too deeply into Janie's past, they could add two and two and make five!'

The two women sat deep in thought. They couldn't be sure of what, if anything Nelson had to do with Jason's death. The fact that his family were of gypsy origin wouldn't help his case with the police.

On the other hand, to be judged because of this would be very unfair, if he was innocent. Plus, there was the baby.

Harriet and Georgina knew at this stage that the police probably did not know about Janie's baby and the association with Nelson, or that Jason and his mates had beaten him up.

Tom came over to the table to take their order for lunch.

'Now ladies what can we tempt you with. The beef is very good or we have a pork roast, also very tasty.'

Georgina decided on the beef as did Harriet.

'It was sad to hear about Janice's partner, Tom. But I don't think he was very nice to her,' Harriet said.

'No, he was a nasty piece of work, Mrs Holt. He was in here shouting his mouth off on Friday. I had to ask him to leave the pub. Think he went to Palmouth. He was in a foul mood and full of drink!'

'He had words with Joe the farmer didn't he?' Georgina asked.

'Yes, and the builders that are doing the barn conversion up the street. It was a wonder they didn't lump him one. That's why I got him out of here.' Tom returned to the bar, to pass the lady's order into the kitchen.

'So not only was Joe angry with Jason but also were those chaps from up the road. I think they come from Palmouth and don't suppose they would have stayed here for long because of driving back to town.'

Harriet looked thoughtful.

'I wonder why Jason stopped at the Streatham house on his way to town?'

'I think we will try and have a chat with that Mandy Streatham. Margaret Sharples lives next door to her. We could easily get her talking, you know what a gossip she is.' Harriet was determined to find out more about Jason's movements after he left the Plough.

The lunch was very good and when they had finished, the women went back to Harriet's for coffee.

They hadn't managed to have a chat with Janice in the pub before they left. It was obvious that she was being kept busy in Tom's kitchen.

'We will go to bingo on Wednesday night. I know Mrs Sharples goes Wednesdays and Fridays, so we should be able to bump into her.'

Georgina agreed.

The Official Investigation

Sergeant Robbins had typed up his interview with Sheryl Davies. He wasn't convinced that she had told him the complete truth about her relationship with Bishop.

Also, although he had not found any flowers at the crime scene, it bothered him that the old girl had mentioned them. He began to think back to his interview in the snug bar with Sheryl and he was beginning to wonder if the old woman had been listening at the door.

It was obvious that Bishop had made enemies. The list of suspects seemed to grow longer every time they interviewed someone new. The men in the Plough, in Gorlstone all hated him, but did they hate him enough to kill him.

The CCTV film had been viewed and it did show Bishop walking up to the newsagents and coming out. Also, it showed Bishop throwing his arms about and obviously shouting at a male person with a pushchair. But the other male did not appear to retaliate but walked off towards the main road and did not go back through the park. This other person had a baseball hat on and the hood of his anorack was over his head, so identification was impossible. The only hope was that someone would come forward who could identify the chap with the baby.

Clive decided to go back to the CCTV film and look at the earlier pictures on the film. But he could not see anything other than a jogger and a couple who had all come forward and been interviewed.

He then decided to look at CCTV film for the minutes after Jason had staggered back onto the path that ran through the park. He saw no-one go or come back along the path.

Inspector Kennedy was due to give a television appeal on local tv that evening.

Again, he was going to ask for witnesses to come forward if they had been anywhere near to Palmouth Park, last Friday, late afternoon or early evening.

Kennedy wasn't convinced that all the statements they had taken contained the whole truth and intended to call a team meeting and insist that all the suspects were asked a lot more questions.

He had a list of questions he needed clarified. He got out his list, and sat trying to make some sense of it all.

Bingo Banter

Harriet and Georgina decided on Wednesday evening to go to bingo in Palmouth.

They purposely got there half an hour before the games were due to start.

As they queued up to buy their tickets, Margaret Sharples entered the bingo hall, and as usual she still had her rollers in her hair covered over by a headscarf.

'Good evening, Margaret,' Georgina said.

Harriet followed suit.

'Unusual to see you two here on a Wednesday,' Margaret said as she was buying her tickets.

'I know, but there is nothing on the telly tonight so we thought we would come to bingo.' Georgina bought two lots of tickets.

'I am going to get a drink for us both, would you like one Margaret?' Harriet said knowing that Margaret was partial to a drink with her bingo.

'Oh that's very nice of you Harriet. I will have a glass of Guinness.'

'You go with Georgina and I will bring the drinks over. Be nice to have a chat.'

Georgina glared at Harriet. The last thing she wanted, was to be stuck with Margaret Sharples for the evening.

Even before they had settled in their seats, Margaret was talking about the murder. So, Georgina encouraged her to talk. By the time Harriet returned with the drinks, she had done a marvellous character assignation on Jason, and quite a few of other local residents. Fortunately, Janie had not been mentioned.

Harriet knew that they only had about fifteen minutes before the games started, so she cut straight to the chase.

'We were told that last Friday night Jason Bishop stopped at your neighbour's house. Was he friendly with Mrs Streatham?'

'Friendly huh! She hated him. He had been hanging around her daughters. I saw him knock on her door that night. They had a few words, then the eldest girl came out of the house and she joined in with the argument. He soon got the message and got back into his wagon and buggered off.'

'Did you hear any of the argument?' Georgina asked.

'I don't make a habit of eavesdropping on my neighbours. All I heard was Mandy telling him to sling his hook and leave her daughters alone. She said he had done enough harm already!'

'Then what happened?' Harriet was aware their time was running out, as the bingo caller was walking to the stage.

'He shot off up the road like a lunatic. Soon after Sarah came out and drove off towards Palmouth in her car. She works in that posh social club down near the harbour.'

The bingo session began, and all chance of chatting was gone.

They knew that there would be a break halfway through the evening and maybe another chance to find out a little more.

In the first session, Margaret managed to win £10, neither Harriet or Georgina came close to a win.

When the break came, Georgina went to the bar for another Guinness for Margaret.

Margaret went off to the ladies and then settled back down to her new glass of Guinness.

'I wonder what Mandy Streatham meant when she said that Bishop had caused enough harm already?' Harriet pondered.

'Well, between you and me, that Jason was seeing Glenys Perry last year. You know Agnes Perry's grand-daughter, that lives in the end cottage on the other side of me. Don't know what happened, but she stopped going out with him and had to go to hospital for an operation. I thought it might have been an abortion or something like that. But she has never been the same since. She never goes out at all now, unless she goes out with Agnes. Agnes won't talk about it and virtually told me to mind my own business. Bloody cheek, as if I was a nosey parker!'

'How could she possibly think that, Margaret. I am sure you were just being neighbourly!'

Harriet said with her tongue in her cheek.

Georgina suppressed a smile. Sometimes Harriet could be a real creep, she thought.

The games began again but none of the ladies were lucky. Harriet got down to needing one number once and got decidedly excited, but to no avail.

They left the bingo hall and found their car.

'Someone told me that Mandy Streatham has two daughters?' Georgina said, as Harriet drove them homewards.

'Yes, she does. Sheryl works in the Park Hotel and Sarah works in that club, as I told you. She goes by the name of Serina, she doesn't like Sarah, thinks it's common,'

Margaret chortled with laughter. 'Thinks she is a hostess but really, she is only a bar maid. She says Serina is more sexy. Daft little bitch.'

'I thought Sheryl's name was Davies,' Harriet said.

'Oh that was her father's name and Sarah's. Mandy was divorced from him years ago. She married again to Richard Streatham, but he died a few weeks ago. They think he was murdered in Palmouth, or they say his death was suspicious at the very least. They haven't buried him yet, the pathologist is still waiting for test results.'

When the bingo session had ended, Harriet offered to give Margaret a lift home, as she thought they might be able to extract more gossip from Margaret, but the extra Guinness seemed to have made sleepy.

They dropped her off outside her house and made their way back to Gorlstone.

'Boy I am shattered, let's talk all this over tomorrow, Georgie. I am going to write it all down. Being a snoop is tiring'

Georgina laughed as Harriet dropped her at the bottom of Cherry Lane. Harriet waited till she saw Georgina reach her gate, and with a wave disappeared up her path to her front door.

Ladies on the Trail

The next day, Georgina walked over to Harriet's house. She had made notes of the conversations they'd had the previous evening.

'Put the kettle on Harry, we need some brain bashing to make some sense of all this.'

'So, Mandy has two daughters. Sarah known as Serina and Sheryl. Jason has been out with Sheryl and the other girl who lives on the other side of Mrs Nosey Parker Sharples!'

'Not that she would listen to her neighbour's conversation of course,' laughed Georgina.

'Perry? Was that the name she said? I couldn't remember.' Harriet always had difficulty with people's names.

'Glenys was the girl's name. I wonder what the operation was for, don't know how we could find out do you?'

'Think we should talk to Sheryl at the Park Hotel, and I wonder if we could get into the Harbour Social Club where the sister works. Perhaps Tim, Janie's friend, would know if you have to belong to the club before we could get in?'

'The disappearing flowers still bother me. We still don't know if the police did find them and it was them that removed them. I will ask the young policeman if we see him. I think Janie said that they were expecting the policeman to visit again. I will keep an eye out for them. I will pop in on some excuse, while he is there,' Harriet said.

'Yes, the flowers are odd. If someone else has moved them, why? Poor Janie must be missing her baby very much. I was wondering if we could give her some money, to go up to Blackpool to find Nelson and Teddy.'

Georgina hated to think about the girl not being with her child.

'Yes, we could, but I think we should be sure that Nelson didn't harm Jason. What about going into Palmarsh this morning, and checking out the Social Club and perhaps popping into the Park Hotel, and hopefully that Sheryl is on duty.'

'Ok, let's go by car as it's a ten minutes' walk from the hotel down to the harbour.'

Harriet found her coat and car keys, and the two women went out to Harriet's car. As they drove out of Ashdown Lane, Harriet spied the young detective just getting out of his car outside Janice's house.

Harriet wound down her window, 'Morning officer. Did you find the bunch of flowers we saw at the crime scene?'

'Harriet, you bugger, you can't ask him here. We are blocking the road!' Georgina whispered to her companion.

Sergeant Robbins walked towards Harriet's car.

'No, we didn't find any flowers. Perhaps you should give me a statement at the station, if you are sure you saw flowers.'

'He doesn't believe you Harry.'

'Of course, officer, we even have a copy of the note that was attached to them.'

With that, Harriet drove off.

'Let him stew on that, the young puppy he thinks we are a pair of nincompoops!'

They drove to Palmouth and went straight down to the harbour. They parked the car and walked along the seafront to the Harbour Social Club.

The doors were open, as the club served meals all day.

'Good morning, ladies,' a rosy cheeked middle aged man greeted them.

'Good morning. Is this place open to non-members or do we have to become members?' Georgina asked.

'There is always someone here who can sign you in. Why don't you come in and see if you like us and I can tell you all about the functions we have here. Then you can make up your minds if you would like to join. We have several activities for the mature member.'

Harriet was about to respond to the hint that he thought they were of an age to sit and dribble, when Georgina poked her in the ribs and said, 'Well thank you, it is very good of you.'

'We are in a bit of a pickle at the moment, staff-wise, as one of our bar maids has not turned up for her shift for the past five days. The younger generation are not like us oldies, irresponsible they are!'

'Oh dear. A girl that lives near us works here we believe. Sarah or Serina I think she is known as.'

'Oh well, she did work here, you are right. But it's her that has gone missing.'

Harriet and Georgina glanced at each but said nothing. They followed their host around the club as he showed them the facilities and he didn't seem to be able to stop talking.

Harriet glanced at her watch and said, 'Oh my goodness, look at the time. I have to be at the dentists in five minutes. Please excuse us, we will return and stay for a drink next time. The time has run away with us. Thank you so much, we are very impressed.'

She grabbed Georgina's arm and made for the door.

'What do you make of that? Serina not been to work for five days. That takes us back to last Saturday, at least. Think we should definitely go and speak to Sheryl, her sister.'

They were both deep in thought, as Harriet drove back up the road to the Park Hotel.

Fortunately, Sheryl was working but she looked very drawn and tired.

'Hello Sheryl, two orange juice and lemonades please. How are you?'

Sheryl did not reply.

Harriet paid for the drinks and Georgina picked up her drink and climbed up onto one of the stools that were by the bar.

'We have just been down to join the Harbour Social Club. The old boy down there told us that your sister hasn't been at work for a few days, hope she isn't ill.'

Georgina was much the more subtle when it came to asking questions.

Sheryl looked shocked at the question.

'Serina hasn't been very well all week,' she said.

'Oh, I am sorry, nothing serious, I hope. There are a lot of bugs going about.'

Sheryl went and picked up some glasses from the other end of the bar.

'She doesn't want to talk about it does she?' Harriet said.

'Here comes Tim, Nelson's friend, perhaps he can throw some light on the subject.

'Hi Tim come and join us. We are going to sit at a table, these bar stools are not good for my back.'

'Or my piles,' whispered Harriet.

Georgina slid from the stool and went over to a table near the bar.

'Any news of Nelson, Tim?' Harriet asked.

'No, nothing. I guess he is with his family. His mother is wonderful with children, Teddy will be fine. I think he will be safer there. If the 'old Bill' connect him to Janie and Jason, they may jump to the wrong conclusion.'

'What do you know about Serina Davies, Sheryl's sister? She has not been at work since last Saturday, it seems odd to us, and Sheryl looks awful. She might talk to you Tim.'

Harriet gave Tim a fiver and told him to get himself a drink.

Tim went to the bar and ordered his drink. He then sat on a bar stool and chatted to Sheryl. She seemed to be happy to be talking to Tim, whereas she had not wanted to speak to Georgina and Harriet.

They tried not to show any interest in the two young people talking at the bar.

It soon became obvious that the conversation had become quite intense, as Sheryl looked as though she wanted to cry. Tim patted her on her arm, and as he left his stool, Sheryl seemed to wipe a tear from her face and then turned to serve another customer who had just come into the pub.

Tim came back to Harriet and Georgina's table.

'I told her that Janie had come to you, and you were trying to help Nelson. She told me that she knew something about Friday night, but she was afraid to say anything. She doesn't know what to do. I told her she should talk to you, and that you wouldn't go the police. Hope that was, ok?'

'She is finishing work at three today. Could she come to your house this afternoon? She knows where you live, as she used to do a paper round in Gorlstone.'

Harriet nodded and smiled over at Sheryl, and gave her the thumbs up.

Tim told them that he would come over to Gorlstone with Sheryl, as he felt she needed some Dutch courage. So, they all left the pub and Harriet and Georgina drove back to their homes, Harriet had to take her dogs for a walk and Georgina had to make some scones, before Sheryl and Tim arrived.

A Confession

At twenty minutes past three, a car drew up outside Georgina's bungalow.

Sheryl and Tim got out and walked up the garden path, Georgina opened her front door. Harriet had arrived ten minutes before.

'Come in you two, Harriet is putting the kettle on.'

Sheryl sat on the settee and Tim sat beside her.

'It's all right Sheryl, Janie trusts Mrs Wright and Mrs Holt. Just tell them what you know about Nelson.'

Harriet came in with a tray, carrying tea and some of Georgina's newly baked scones.

She handed a plate to Sheryl and Tim and told them to help themselves.

'Now Sheryl, what is worrying you love, if we can help, we will do so.'

Sheryl got out her hanky from her bag and said, 'On Friday night, Jason called at our house. I was already at work at the Park Hotel. He wanted to speak to Sarah. We still call her Sarah, but my mother told him to bugger off, excuse my language!

'She didn't like Jason. My step-father had warned him off pestering both me and Sarah. I hated him for what happened to Glenys, that's our next-door neighbour.'

'What did happen to Glenys, Sheryl?' Georgina asked.

'Glenys was potty about Jason last year. I don't know why, but she really had a thing for him. He started to take her out and promised her he would get her a job as a dancer, in some club of a mate of his in Southampton.

'We told her not to get involved with him, as he knew some really rough blokes. But she wouldn't listen. She told us after, that she had been asked to do some modelling, but she had to go and have a makeover at some posh beauty clinic. She seemed very excited.'

Harriet poured out the tea and handed the cups around.

69

'Glenys went off with Jason last November and we didn't see her for about a couple of weeks. The next we knew, Glenys came back home and she wouldn't see anyone.

'She went into hospital soon after, no-one knew why. Her mother told us nothing and got very stroppy when we asked. When she came home again, I went round to see her, took her some chocolates. Her mother let me in. Glenys looked awful. She was still in pyjamas even though it was afternoon.

'I asked her about Jason and she burst into tears, then her mother then asked me to go. As I went out, she told me that Glenys wasn't seeing him anymore and that Glenys was suffering with a nervous breakdown. We assumed that Jason had dumped her and that was what had caused the breakdown.'

'So, was all this before or after he went out with you?'

'It wasn't me he went out with it, it was Sarah, my sister. I lied to the police, as I didn't want them to go and question Sarah. It was before he took up with Glenys. She told him to get lost when he asked her to go and work in this club in Southampton, that was when he hit her. So, she kept well clear of him from then on.

'It was Sarah he called round to see when mum was at bingo, not me. But I told the police it was me he came to see. It was after that visit that my step-dad said he was going to have a word with him to stay away from us.'

'Where is Sarah now? We know she hasn't been to work since last Friday night,' Harriet said.

Sheryl looked at Tim and tears came to her eyes.

'I can't tell you, it's safer that way!'

'Now look Sheryl, it's obvious that you are afraid of something or someone. Anything you tell us will go no further. We understand you know something about Nelson, and poor Janie is beside herself with worry,' Georgina said very quietly.

Tim nodded at Sheryl, 'Go on tell Mrs Wright, Nelson is my mate I am worried about him as well.'

Sheryl wiped her eyes and continued.

'After Jason came to our house last Friday night, Sarah got a phone call from her work. One of the girls hadn't turned up and they asked her if she could go in and help them out. Friday nights are usually busy. So, she got in her car soon after Jason had left and drove into Palmouth. On the nights that we both worked, Sarah would leave her car in the car-park at my work, and as I finished about half an hour earlier than her, I would drive her car down to the Harbour Social Club and pick her up. I had gone into work on the bus as I worked all day that Friday, I was going to catch the last bus home.

'She phoned me just as she was leaving home to tell me she would be leaving her car for me to pick her up. After she had parked her car in the Park Hotel car-park, she was going to take a short cut across the park to the Harbour club. She told me that as she walked through the park, she met Jason. He grabbed hold of her and started to shout at her about her refusal to renew their arrangement as he put it.'

'Then what happened love?' Harriet said.

'She struggled with him and when he wouldn't let go of her, she hit him in the face with her handbag. She forgot that she had put a bottle of coke in her bag and she told me that her bag caught Jason right on his nose, which started a nose bleed. He fell backwards and hit his head on the metal park seat. She said he staggered onto the grass and then fell down. She just ran as fast as she could back out of the park.

'That was when she met Nelson who was walking up the main road from the shops. He was pushing a pushchair. He stopped her and asked her what was the matter, as she was crying. She told him that she thought she had killed a man in the park.'

'So, Nelson did walk back up the main road and not walked back through the park,' Tim said.

'So go on Sheryl, what happened next?' The women were gripped by the tale.

'Nelson went back into the park with Sarah, and when he saw it was Jason that she had hit, he felt for a pulse in his neck. He told Sarah not to worry as Jason wasn't dead and they should get away as quickly as possible, before he came round. So, Sarah said they ran back to the main road. When they got there, Nelson told her to take off her cardigan as there was blood on it.

'She said that he took the cardigan and told her he would get rid of it. He told her to go to work via the main road and say nothing to anyone. Which she did, and that was the last she saw of Nelson. The next day, when we heard that Jason's body had been found in the park, she freaked out. She has gone where they won't be able to find her. He was a horrible man and she didn't mean to kill him.'

Sheryl burst out into floods of tears.

'But Nelson said he felt a pulse therefore he wasn't dead,' Tim said.

'But he must have died after Sarah and Nelson left him!' Sheryl said through her sobs.

Georgina looked horrified. This was serious.

Harriet took Sheryl's hand, 'Now listen. We don't know what Jason died of. The bash he got on his head, when he fell against the tree could have killed him but not necessarily. I think we should try and find out what the post-mortem says about, the cause of death.'

'How are you explaining Sarah's disappearance?' Georgina asked.

'I phoned her work and told them she was poorly. But she told my mum that she was going to see her friend in Hastings for a few days. She went on Saturday morning, after we heard about Jason. She was so scared.'

'So, Nelson took Sarah's cardigan and no-one has seen him since?' Tim looked puzzled.

'Yes, he told Sarah that he would burn it and not to tell anyone that she had been near the park that night.' Sheryl seemed a little calmer.

Harriet poured them all another cup of tea.

'Well Sarah can't stay away for too long, that will look suspicious. I presume you are in contact with her. We will try and find out the details of the post-mortem. Janie told us that the police said it would be better for Jason's brother to identify him, as it wasn't a pleasant sight. So just knocking into the park bench couldn't have done that much damage, could it?' As usual, Georgina was the voice of reason.

'Be best if you act normally. If the police want to speak to Sarah, just say she is staying with a girlfriend for a few days, and will be back soon. There is no reason for them to look for Sarah at the moment. They think it was you that he was chasing after, not Sarah, so keep it like that at the moment.'

'Yes, I agree,' Harriet said. 'And try not to worry too much.'

Tim and Sheryl finished their tea and then left. Sheryl was feeling not so panic stricken, as she had been when she first came to Georgina's bungalow.

'Thank you, Mrs Wright and Mrs Holt it has helped to talk to someone.'

'Please call us Georgina and Harriet. We will keep in touch. Leave us your mobile telephone number and yours too, Tim. We will try and find out a bit more and then we will let you know and try not to worry.'

When they had gone, Harriet took the cups to the kitchen and Georgina came and together they washed up.

'What do you think Georgie?'

'I think we will have to try and see the results of the post-mortem. I suppose if Jason had a thin skull, it is possible that the bang on the park seat could have killed him. But not necessarily.'

Both of them wanted to have a think about the situation.

'I am just going to get my newspaper on my way home, then have a quiet evening. I will see you tomorrow,' Harriet said, as she got up to go home.

Mushrooming and a Rabbit called Houdini

'What about going to Bingo tonight? Think Mandy Streatham goes on Friday,' Harriet said, the following morning, as they sat in Georgina's kitchen.

'I was thinking that myself, but we don't want to get lumbered with Margaret Sharples again, do we?' Georgina shuddered. 'I know we got information out of her, but it's Mandy we need to talk to now. That Margaret, I think she chews pickled onions, her breath smells dreadful, and she spits when she speaks to you.'

Harriet laughed.

'And her false teeth jump up and down when she talks!'

'I would like to see what flowers are growing in the Streatham's garden, perhaps we can take a walk this morning. I did try to look as we drove back from town but there are no flowers in any of the front gardens in those cottages where Sheryl's lives.'

Harriet said, 'We should have asked her, but I expect she wants to keep as far away as possible from the scene of the crime. So, I don't think it was her.'

Georgina was sitting, trying to visualise the gardens at the cottages where the Streatham's lived.

'The flowers were not shop bought. Looked as though someone had picked them from their garden, or someone else's. I wished I had taken a photo of them'.

'Well, we couldn't hang around there, could we? So, don't beat yourself up, Sherlock.'

Georgina knew Harriet was right.

They talked about going on the walk, and agreed that the cottages were probably a good mile along the road to Palmouth. They decided to take one of the cars and park in a lay-by a little way from the cottages.

'Better put wellies on, as we will have to go into the field behind the cottage. There is a gate just up the road from the cottages, we can climb over, and wander round the back of the houses.'

Georgina went and found her wellington boots and Harriet went back to her house to find hers. Georgina said she would drive over and pick her up on the main road.

Georgina was already waiting for Harriet when she came out of her house wearing her yellow wellies.

'What do we say if anyone sees us?' Georgina asked.

'Mushrooming!' Harriet said.

'It's too late for mushrooms, what about collecting rabbit food?'

'We haven't got a rabbit. Suppose we could invent one!'

'Only you could invent a rabbit Harry, what is our rabbit called?' Georgina said, laughing.

'Houdini, then if anyone asks to see him, we can say he has escaped!'

They both laughed.

The lay-by was empty, fortunately, so Georgina was able to park the car. The two women got out of the car. Georgina locked the doors, and they walked up the road towards the five barred gate, that led into the fields that ran behind the row of cottages, where the Streatham's lived.

Georgina as usual, had worn a skirt.

'Are you going to be able to get your leg over the gate?' Harriet asked her friend.

Georgina put her foot on the bottom bar of the gate and started to climb up.

'I should have put trousers on,' she said, as she tried to get her leg over the top of the gate.

As she straddled the gate, Harriet gave her a gentle push. Georgina toppled over and landed in a heap, on the field.

'Thanks mate, is that revenge for me shoving you through that window?' She said, as she struggled up. Harriet climbed over and pulled Georgina to her feet.

'Sorry, I thought you needed some help.'

The two women started to walk along the hedgerow and reached the six-foot fencing that ran along the side of the gardens. They followed the fencing, till they got to the rear of the cottages.

'There might be a hole in the fence, which we can look through. These interwoven panels sometimes warp, and it`s possible to see through the cracks.'

Georgina suddenly pointed to a slit in the woodwork.

They both peered through, into the Streatham's garden.

'Well, there isn't any flowers in there. Looks like they grow only veg,' Harriet said.

They walked on and got to the back of Margaret Sharples house. This didn't present a viewing problem, as her boundary was a privet hedge. They pulled the branches of the hedge apart, and saw a moth eaten lawn and a washing line adorned with several pairs of baggy knickers, woollen vests, and two flannel night dresses, but no flowers.

They then walked on to the third house, only to find another six-foot wooden fence. This fence seemed impenetrable. There were no holes or warped bits. Harriet found a knot in the wood and tried to dislodge it, but it wasn't going to budge.

Georgina noticed a metal water trough, a couple of yards from the fence. She went over to it and tried to wriggle it nearer to the fence.

Harriet came over and helped her, and between them they got the trough beside the fence. It still had some water in it, which had made it heavier.

It was decided, that as Georgina was the lightest, she should be the one to balance on the trough and peep over the fence.

She held onto Harriet's shoulder for balance and got one foot on either side of the trough and was just able to see into Agnes Perry's garden.

'Eureka,' she said, then lost her balance. One foot went into the water in the trough and she tumbled backwards knocking into Harriet, and they both ended up in a heap on the ground.

'Eureka, bloody what? Listen, someone is coming.' Harriet got to her feet, pulling a bedraggled Georgina to her feet, just as a large black Labrador came bounding round the corner, followed by a grey-haired woman.

'Good afternoon, quite nice now,' Harriet said.

She patted the dog, who seemed very friendly.

Georgina started to pick some wild parsley and put it in a plastic carrier bag, that she had found in her anorak pocket.

'Bunny rabbit food for Houdini, our rabbit,' she said, and carried on looking around at the ground.

'My rabbit is fed on pellets, can't be bothered to go foraging,' the old woman said, eying Georgina up, as the muddy water dripped off her coat where she had fallen.

'Are you Margaret's neighbour?' Harriet asked, trying to divert the woman's attention from her muddy friend, 'We go to bingo with her.'

'Yes unfortunately, the woman is a nosy old bat!'

This was obviously Agnes Perry, mother of the ex-girlfriend of Jason.

'We gathered that and we do try to avoid sitting too close to her,' Georgina said, returning with a handful of dandelion leaves.

'She had a lot to say about that man that was murdered in the park in Palmouth, I think that was awful. Then I hear, he wasn't a very nice man,' Harriet said, trying to draw the woman into conversation.

'Pure evil,' the woman said, and abruptly whistled her dog and plodded off across the field.

'What did you see in her garden Georgie, before you leapt off the trough?'

'Her garden is lovely and has loads of marigolds all-round the borders. That's not all, if you look round the corner, the fence has a prolific climbing plant on it and intertwined is a large amount of deadly nightshade!'

Harriet gasped, 'That must be where the flowers came from. If the daughter was keen on Jason and he dropped her, perhaps she took the flowers into the park, and I reckon if the mother realised what she had done she would be the one to remove them.'

'Good thinking Sherlock. But how do we prove it, and what relevance has it got to who murdered him?'

They walked back to the field gate, only to find there was no need to climb over, as the gate was slightly ajar, probably left like that by Mrs Perry. As there didn't appear to be any livestock in the field, they went through and left the gate as they had found it, as Agnes Perry was at the top of the field and making her way back to the road. They gave her a wave and took the carrier bag of rabbit food back to the car.

'What are we going to do with this then?' Georgina asked.

'We could eat the dandelion leaves; they say they are edible.'

'Humph! You can if you like, but they say they make you wet the bed!' Georgina said laughing.

'Here, give the bag to me.' Harriet opened her window and threw the contents of the bag out of the window. A very surprised sheep in the field by the road, was suddenly enveloped by Houdini's dinner. Harriet shook the bag out of the window then brought it back in and folded it up. 'Not throwing that away, they cost five pence now!'

'How do we get to speak to Glenys and we need to find out the results of the post mortem?' Georgina said.

'Think it may be put it in the newspaper, when it's completed. They seem to be taking a long time. I think we should go and see that policeman and tell him what was written on the card left with flowers. Then perhaps we can get some information on how the investigation is going.'

'Ok, good idea Harry, but let's go to Bingo tonight and try to talk to Mandy Streatham.'

Cat-Nap

It was getting on, for five when Harriet left Georgina's.

Gorlstone was a quiet village, but at about this time, the shop usually had a rush of last-minute customers. Those who had been at work, called in for their newspapers and something for their tea.

The official closing time was five-thirty, but it was usually six, before Brian Martindale locked the shop door. Both he and Penny his wife loved a natter with all their customers. If anyone needed to know anything, then Brian and Penny were the people to ask.

As Harriet walked in, she heard Penny talking to old Jim Talbot.

Jim lived on the main street in the end house of a terrace of old Victorian cottages. No-one actually knew how old Jim was, but it was well known that he had been born and raised in the cottage where he lived.

He had spent his working life away from Gorlstone and returned with his wife when he retired, to live in his parental home, after his parents had died. He was now a widower.

He seemed to remember the wars, and some of the things he told people, made you really wonder just how old he was. Some said his father had fought in the first world war and he definitely had some amazing stories to tell.

Harriet enjoyed talking to the old man and had often sat on the chairs outside the shop with him, just to listen to his tales.

'Hello Jim and Penny,' she said, as she went to find her paper. She picked up a few other bits and pieces that she knew she needed. Harriet liked to support the local shop when she could, as many villages were losing their little shops. All the villagers felt the same.

'Oh, Jim that is awful. What a little brat. When she comes in here with her mother, she stamps her feet till her mother gives her some sweets. Mind you, Mrs Hoity Toity doesn't shop here only when she has to. Never says please or thank you.'

'I bet I can guess who you are talking about!' Brian appeared from the back room.

'Her from 'The Gables, right am I?' He said laughing.

Jim nodded, 'Just telling your missus. They got one of them fluffy cats, a pretty thing it is too. That child torments that animal something awful. Puts dresses on it and then drags it around the garden. When it scratches her, she kicks it.'

'Little bitch, if you said anything to her mother, she wouldn't like it.' Penny said.

'I did say to her ladyship that the kid was abusing the cat, do you know what she said? 'It's only a cat and it should learn not to scratch my daughter'.'

Harriet was horrified. She was an animal lover and the thought of an animal being abused in that way, was dreadful.

'Don't know what can be done, I am sure, perhaps the puss will run away.' Jim picked up his groceries and went to leave the shop.

Harriet said, 'Hang on a minute Jim.' She paid for her goods and followed Jim out of the shop door.

'I can't bear the thought of that poor cat Jim. Does the cat sleep indoors at night?' She asked.

'No, it lives in the shed in the garden. It's only let out when the child wants to play with it. It's got a cage inside the shed. My son does the lawn for her mother and he has to empty the cat litter tray, she's too high and mighty to get her hands dirty. My boy says the cats a lovely creature.'

'Is there a back entrance to the Gable's Garden?' Harriet asked.

'No, only fields behind, and big six-foot fence all along the back,' Jim said thoughtfully. 'Why, are you planning kidnap the cat Harriet?'

'Cat-nap, perhaps!' Harriet's brain was wondering if the ladder in Georgina's garage would be long enough for her to climb into The Gable's Garden. Then she thought about how she would then get back over the fence with a cat.

Jim scratched his head. He could see that Harriet was turning the situation over in her head.

'Well before the Johnson-Hargreaves moved into the Gables, old Mrs Fanshawe lived there. Me and my missus used to look after her. We had a gate made years ago at the bottom of our garden, so that we didn't have to go all the way round to get into see Mrs Fanshawe. Nice old dear she was too.'

Harriet's eyes lit up.

'Is the gate still there Jim?'

'Oh yes. I took the handles off on the Gables side and bolted it on my side. The ivy has grown over it a bit now, don't suppose her ladyship even knows it's there.'

'Is there a security light in the back of the house?' Harriet asked.

'Yes, there is, don't know how far down the garden, the beam goes though. What are you planning, young woman?' Jim laughed, and Harriet smiled.

'Let me think about this for a while. What day does your son mow the grass at the Gables, Jim?'

'He is doing it on Saturday morning, as Mrs Johnson-Hargreaves is having a luncheon party on Sunday.'

'Could you ask him to switch off the security light when he goes there, or if he can't, could he point it away from the garden shed?' Harriet was getting quite excited.

Jim grinned, 'There is no way her ladyship allows a mere gardener into her house. The switch is somewhere inside. But I will get him to swivel the light to the other side of the garden.'

'I will come round Saturday evening. If you can remove the ivy from the old gate, so we can go that way into the Gables Garden. I will bring Georgina with me; this will be a two-man job.'

'No, a three-man job my dear. We will rescue that poor puss cat. But what happens when we have him.'

'Don't you worry about that. One thing at a time.'

Two Little Ducks

Friday evening, Harriet and Georgina went to Bingo. They decided to go in Georgina's car, as Margaret knew what Harriet's car looked like. They decided to park at the back of the car park at the Bingo Hall and hope that they had avoided her. They purposefully waited in the foyer. That way, they hoped to join the queue when Mandy Streatham arrived. Fortunately, they saw Margaret come in and hid behind a large slot machine, while she bought her tickets and disappeared into the hall.

They didn't have to wait long. Mandy came in with a, tall, dark haired young woman. Georgina and Harriet joined the queue behind Mandy.

'We were hiding behind the slot machine, as we didn't want to get lumbered with that woman who comes to bingo in her rollers!'

Mandy turned round and laughed. 'You must mean my awful neighbour!'

'Oh do you live in the cottages on the Gorlstone road?' Georgina said innocently.

'Yes, sadly she lives next door, a right nosy one she is too.' Mandy said. 'We wish she would move somewhere else, don't we Glenys.'

'Bingo,' thought Harriet.

'Oh Gosh, you must be Mrs Streatham, who sadly lost your husband recently. I am so sorry it was very sad. We live in Gorlstone and I am afraid news travels fast.'

'Yes, I think I have seen you both in the Plough on a Sunday. My husband often took me for a Sunday lunch. I do miss him.'

'We are both widows, so we know how you feel. If ever you are in the village do call in have a cup of tea. I live behind the old bakery, and Georgina lives in the first bungalow in Cherry Lane. I am Harriet and my friend is Georgina.'

Mandy was quite touched by the friendly pair of old ladies. People had seemed to shy away from her and didn't know what to say, so it was nice to talk to them both, especially as they had shared the loss of their husbands.

They got their tickets and followed Mandy through the doors into the hall. 'That Mrs Sharples is sitting over on the right, so we will go over here away from her,' Harriet said loudly.

'Yes, so will we, come on Glenys, we will follow Harriet and Georgina.'

They all settled down in adjacent seats and got out their dabbers, ready for the Bingo to start.

During the first session, Glenys won a house but neither Harriet, Georgina or Mandy won anything.

At the interval, Mandy said, 'That was beginners' luck, well done Glenys. That should cheer you up.'

'Were you feeling a little sad then Glenys?' Harriet asked.

Mandy patted Glenys on the shoulder, 'Yes Glenys hasn't been too well, but she is slowly getting there, aren't you pet?'

Glenys smiled and asked where the toilets were and got up to go.

'Think I will go too, wait for me Glenys.' Georgina followed the girl.

'She looks a nice lass,' Harriet said.

'Yes, she lives on the other side of Margaret, in the end house. She had a bit of boyfriend trouble. He was a bad lot. Got her entangled with some bad people. You may have heard about the man they found in the park last week. That was the man she was keen on; she hates him now. But think her health will improve, the doctors are hopeful. I thought a night at Bingo would perk her up.'

'Oh, dear poor lamb. Did she get pregnant?'

'Oh no, he got her involved in all this breast enhancement nonsense. She wanted to be a model, you know, a proper one that shows off clothes, not one of those sex kittens. Told her she had to have breast implants as she was too flat chested. Took her to one of these clinics out near, Darrington and they made a right mess up of it, made her really ill. Look she is coming back, please say nothing, probably shouldn't have told you.'

'Won't say a word Mandy.' Georgina thought, that there was another possibility for wanting Jason dead.

The evening passed pleasantly. Harriet won a tenner on a line and Mandy won twenty on a two liner.

Georgina and Harriet said goodbye to Mandy and Glenys and went to find their car, being careful to avoid Margaret Sharples.

'Well, that was interesting, old bean,' Georgina said. 'Did you get anything out of Glenys?

'Not much. I didn't want to seem to be prying. She did tell me, that her mother had told her that two stupid women had been collecting rabbit food in the field behind their house, and one of them had fallen in a water trough. She said her mother had tried not to laugh, as they stood there dripping and pretending nothing had happened!'

'Oops. Stupid women eh!' Georgina laughed.

Georgina repeated her conversation with Mandy, and both thought that this was something else that the police didn't know about.

'We will have to sit down and think all this out tomorrow,' Georgina said.

'Oh tomorrow, we have another problem to solve. Another case, this could be an Inspector Clouseau type adventure,' Harriet told her mystified friend.

'Not another toilet window job I hope!'

'Well, not quite. I will explain on the way home,' Harriet said, hoping Georgina wouldn't go through the roof at her plan.

Cat-Nap, Part Two

Georgina had listened to Harriet's tale about the molestation of the Johnson-Hargreaves's cat with horror. Partly on the side of the cat, and partly worried where the conversation was going and what hair-brained scheme Harriet might be cooking up.

By the time they had arrived at Gorlstone, Georgina was convinced that some action had to be taken. She wasn't too sure that Harriet's plan was fool proof, especially as she had been elected to take a major role in the action.

The plan was for Georgina (as she was the skinny one) to go through the gate at the bottom of Jim's garden. Go to the shed and rescue the cat.

What could go wrong?

They were going to wait till it was dark. The security light was to be moved by Jim's son, so if it did come on, it should be pointing away from the garden shed.

The cat hopefully wouldn't be missed till the following morning and Georgina was to leave the shed door ajar, so it would be thought that the cat had escaped.

They had decided that black clothes should be worn. Harriet said she would black Georgina's face up, but Georgina drew the line at that.

When she arrived at Harriet's on Saturday evening, she was given a black balaclava and black gloves. The women laughed like a couple of children. 'We could take up bank robbery I suppose, if we get desperate.'

'Just poke the balaclava and gloves in your pocket. Glad you wore trousers, wouldn't want you to catch your drawers on anything.'

They locked Harriet's house up, crossed the road and walked up to Jim's cottage and tapped on his front door.

Jim was waiting for them. Georgina could see that the old man was quite excited about the escapade.

'I have pulled the ivy away from the old gate, but left it so we can put it back again after.' Jim told the women. 'It's not yet quite dark.'

As they stood in Jim's back garden, they heard a child scream, 'Get in your shed, you stupid cat.'

They stood up on the wall on Jim's side of the fence and watched as the child grabbed hold of the cat's tail and dragged the animal into the shed and slammed the shed door.

'You're not getting any dinner now for scratching me.' She kicked the door and stomped back to the house and slammed the house door.

Harriet felt near to tears and any doubts that Georgina had before, disappeared. They went back into Jim's house to wait until it got darker.

'The security light seemed to be pointing to the side of the garden, so that's ok. My son said he had turned it as far as he could, to the left-hand side.'

Jim offered the women a small glass of sherry, a tipple he was very fond of. They sipped their drink and watched as it got darker.

'Right Mrs Bond, time for action,' Harriet said.

They donned the balaclavas and gloves. Jim put on his Sherlock Holmes style cap, which made the girls laugh. They closed Jim's back door and crept quietly up his garden, but when Harriet fell over a bucket, there was a clatter. They all stood still, but heard no movement from the other side of the fence. Jim pushed back the bolt on the wooden gate, that was almost hidden in the hedgerow.

They peered into the Johnson-Hargreaves Garden. The shed was about halfway up on the opposite side of the garden.

'I would go slowly girl and keep low; in case the censors pick you up. We don't know how far round the light could show, if you do set it off,' Jim whispered to Georgie.

'Good luck,' Harriet said.

Georgina stepped into the next-door garden. She bent down as low as her arthritic hip would allow, and slowly went along the path that ran along the end of the garden. She suddenly heard a rustling in the bushes, she froze. A startled hedgehog snorted on to the path in front of her, and scuttled across the lawn. Georgina carried on, turned the corner, went up the other side of the lawn and got to the shed. She undid the bolt on the shed door and slipped inside.

'It's alright pussy,' she whispered. She bent down and found the cage. She suddenly heard the cat start to purr.' Puss, puss it's really ok don't be scared.' She opened the cage and suddenly the cat came out and was rubbing round her legs. She stroked the cat and picked him up and was about to make for the door, when she heard a noise. She stepped back and squatted behind a mower, still holding the cat.

'Damned child, can't she do anything right. The bloody shed door has been left open. You still there, you horrible feline.'

Georgina meowed very quietly. The door was then slammed shut and Georgina heard the bolt being slid into place.

'Oh shit,' she thought.

Jim and Harriet had seen someone coming out of the house after Georgina had disappeared into the shed. They watched horrified, as Alicia Johnson-Hargreaves strode up the path, and watched helplessly, as she closed the shed door.

She went back up to the house and shouted, 'Oliver come here, the security light has got twisted around and its only shining on one side of the garden. I nearly fell over one of the gnomes.' Her husband grumbled, but came out with a step-ladder and climbed up and realigned the light. That done, they both went back indoors.

Jim and Harriet were horrified. 'What do we do now?' Jim asked anxiously.

'There's only thing we can do.' With that, Harriet pulled her balaclava down over her face and crawled through the gate. She moved very slowly, hoping the sensor wouldn't spot her. She got to the far side of the garden. Her knees were killing her, as she crawled. She slowed her crawl down and flattened herself to the floor, almost sliding up the path. As she got closer to the shed, she whispered, 'Georgie, can you hear me?'

Georgina was sitting on the floor by the door, cuddling the ecstatic cat and had heard the sliding noise that Harriet was making as she slid up the path.

'Yes, let me out,' she whispered.

'Look if the bloody light comes on, we will just have to run for it, have you got the cat?'

'Yes, can't you hear it purring?'

Just then, the sensor picked up Harriet and the garden was illuminated. She slid back the bolt on the shed door, and Georgie, cat and Harriet ran back down the garden and through the wooden gate into Jim's garden. Harriet closed the gate and locked it and she pushed the ivy back into place. Jim was no-where to be seen. They ran up Jim's garden path, missing the bucket this time and into his kitchen. Jim reappeared from his front door. 'Where you been Jim?' Harriet asked.

The old man looked red in the face and he had to sit down. 'Had to create a diversion when I saw that damned light come back on my lovelies! Went to tell Mrs Thing next door, that some rascal had put a brick through their BMW's window on their drive. Real upset they was, real shame wasn't it, but it got them out of their house!'

The two women laughed, 'Oh Jim you didn't, did you?'

The old man laughed and took his gloves off, 'Not had so much fun for years! Now you had better disappear with that moggy before the boys in blue arrive to catch the dastardly criminal that vandalised their precious car.'

They left Jim's house and trotted round to Georgina's with the cat tucked up in Georgina's anorak, purring so loudly, they just hoped that they didn't meet anyone.

The Johnson-Hargreaves were in their driveway, surveying the damage to their car, so they didn't see the women leave Jim's house.

When they got into Georgina's bungalow, she took the still loudly purring cat out of her coat into the warm kitchen. She had gone out to her garage earlier that day and retrieved the basket, litter tray and food bowls that she had been loath to throw away, after her beloved Tootsie had died. She had sworn she would never have another cat, as the heartbreak it had caused when she died was too much to bear. She had also found half a bag of wood litter pellets for the tray and had set it all up in the kitchen ready. The fluffy basket had got lovely and warm beside her Aga.

She put the cat on the floor and opened a can of cat food that Harriet had brought over, which she had in her cupboard for her cats.

The cat was long haired and pure white. Georgina had felt a lot of lumps of matted fur as she had carried the animal. It was obvious that no-one had ever groomed the cat.

Puss gobbled up the food ravenously, purring between mouthfuls.

'What now,' Georgie asked Harriet. 'There will be a hue and cry when they discover he is gone!'

'Well, we left the door open, so they will assume that he has got out, although she will say that she bolted the door.'

Georgina sat in her little armchair she kept by her Aga and the cat jumped up onto her lap, rubbed himself all round her, purring again.

'He is lovely, but how can I keep him, living so close to his previous home.'

Harriet was thinking. 'Let's see what sort of stink they kick up. They will probably be more concerned about her BMW than the cat. He seems happy enough to be here and he could become a house cat. Let's wait till the morning and play it by ear, see if he settles, poor little man.'

Harriet gave the now sleeping cat a stroke as he lay curled up on Georgina's lap, put her coat on and left her friend cuddling her new friend.

As Harriet made her way back to her house, she saw a police car pull into the Johnson-Hargreaves driveway. She hoped old Jim would be alright. She had a little smile to herself as crossed the road. The old man had thoroughly enjoyed the whole escapade.

Georgina laid the cat into the warm basket and got her pyjamas on and got into bed. She had just turned the light off in her bedroom, when she was aware of her door creaking open and in walked the cat. He jumped up on her bed purring loudly, he walked round in a circle and curled up next to Georgina.

'Oh, so this is where you are going to sleep at night, is it?' She said, giving the cat a stroke and they both promptly went to sleep.

The next morning, Harriet arrived to find Georgina sitting in the same chair as she had been when Harriet left the night before.

'Have you sat there all night?'

'No, we are just having a post-breakfast cuddle. His lordship came and curled up on my bed with me. I haven't been sleeping very well as you know, but last night I slept like a log.'

'It looks as though the cat is going to stay then. What are you going to call him?'

Georgina hadn't had to think too long about that question, 'Houdini, of course,' she said laughing.' 'But Dino, for short.'

'So, your imaginary rabbit has turned into a moggy.' They both laughed.

'I am going to cut all those lumps of fur out of his coat and possibly give him a trim. I may have to put some colour on him to disguise him a bit as well. What do you think?'

Harriet tried to think what she had in her cupboard at home.

'I have some henna powder. Wonder what colour he would come out if we used that. But not sure if it is toxic to animals. Think I will stick to gravy browning, can't use a human hair dye, as they may be toxic when he licks his fur.'

Georgina was laughing, 'You dopey woman, gravy browning. Suppose we could call him Bisto.'

The women set to and cut out the matted fur from the cat. He seemed to think it a good game, purring all the time. They trimmed his fur all over, realizing just how thin the animal was, under all his fur.

'It's disgraceful, they can't have been feeding him properly at all. He has eaten two tins this morning already. We will have to go to town to get a good supply in. I can't suddenly start buying cat food from Martindales, as they know I haven't got a cat.'

When they had trimmed Dino up, he looked very different. Georgina brushed him gently which he seemed to like. He then climbed into his basket by the fire and went to sleep.

'We will pop into Tesco's this morning as I need a few things as well. Are we getting extra gravy browning as well?' Harriet said. 'I will get my paper later and see if the shop has heard anything about the events of last night.' Harriet said.

'Ok, he seems happy enough to be here, so let's hope Mrs Johnson-Hargreaves' daughter doesn't kick up too much fuss, the little hussy!'

The Clinic

After the two women had been shopping, they sat in Georgina's kitchen. The cat was still been in his basket when they came through the front door. As soon as he heard Georgina, he leapt out of the basket and rushed up to Georgie, rubbed all round her and Harriet's legs, purring as usual.

He made no attempt to go out of the front door, as the women had entered and followed them back into the kitchen. Georgina opened one of the tins she had bought in town, and Dino eagerly ate from his bowl.

He then stretched himself and climbed back into his basket and with a big sigh went back to sleep.

'Now we decide what we do about the Jason Bishop affair. I was thinking about our visit to the garden centre. Do you remember when the ladies nearly fell into the pond?'

Georgina was making the tea and she nodded her head. 'The woman who were talking about breast implants? Yes, I remember, I can see where you are going with this—the Glenys Perry situation?'

Harriet took her cup of tea from Georgina.

'I was looking at the notice board in the café while you were paying the bill. I am sure I saw an advertisement for a health clinic on there.'

'We could go over there and see if it's still there. Perhaps the two women had put it there.'

Dino was still sleeping happily, so they decided to take a run over to the garden centre. It was a twenty minutes ride in the car. They went straight into the café and looked at the notice board.

'Look, there it is. Darrington Manor. Cosmetic surgery procedures, breast implants etc. It's got to be the place that young Glenys went to.'

'I'll take the telephone number and the post code. We could go and have a look. Why don't we make an enquiry about having a procedure.'

91

Georgina shuddered. 'You are joking, neither of us need breast implants. No Harriet, not another daft idea.'

But Harriet was plotting in her head, and Georgina could see it by the thoughtful expression on her face.

They put the post code into Georgina's satellite navigation and followed the instructions. It took over three quarters of an hour before they reached the village of Darrington. There were decorative signs for Darrington Manor in the village, pointing on the road leading out of the village, which they followed. A few hundred yards from the village centre, they saw the large sign outside a driveway. Georgina drove up the tarmac road to the large imposing red-brick, Georgian-style house. She stopped the car and before she could say anything, Harriet had opened the door and went up the stone steps to the front door. She rang the bell and before Georgina could get out of the car, the door was opened and Harriet disappeared inside. All Georgina could do was get back into the car and wait for her dotty friend!

Once inside, Harriet found herself in a capacious hallway. There was a very ornate reception desk attended by the young woman who had opened the front door for Harriet. There was a huge chandelier hanging above the stairway that ascended from the hallway, and magnificent paintings were adorning the walls up the stairs.

'Good afternoon, madam, how can I help you?'

Suddenly Harriet became aware that she was dressed in jeans and trainers and compared to the obvious designer wear that the young woman was wearing, she looked a real scruff!

'Please excuse my attire, my stockman has taken ill, and I have had to organise the deer herd on the estate today, a real pain my dear.'

'Oh, please don't apologise. How can we help you?'

Harriet was looking at a brochure on the reception desk. 'I was thinking of a face lift and a tummy tuck. Have you any brochures to let me know what these would entail. Perhaps I could have tour of your facilities and a chat with your surgeon, before I make up my mind.'

'I can make you an appointment, and here is a price list of procedures and it will also tell you some information about us.'

Harriet took the brochures, 'Who owns this place now? My husband's family owned this house many years ago. He is Lord Frobisher.'

The girl looked impressed.

'The owners are the Carbury sisters. They are beauticians who studied in America…' Just then, a woman came down the stairs looking angry. Harriet recognised her as one of the women they had seen in the garden centre.

'Letticia, you are needed upstairs.' Harriet got the impression that perhaps Letticia was in trouble for telling her something she shouldn't.

'This is Lady Frobisher, Miss Carbury, I have given her a brochure.'

Harriet thought it time she abandoned ship. She glanced at her watch and said, 'My goodness, I must fly. I have the feed in the car for the herd. I have your contact number; I will call to make an appointment tomorrow. Thank you, Letticia. You have been so helpful.' With that, she turned and went out of the door as quickly as possible, hoping that Miss Carbury would not recognise her from the garden centre.

Georgina was beginning to wonder what was keeping Harriet and was pleased to see her skip down the steps.

'Drive, Georgie quick!'

'Oh my God, what have you done?'

Harriet started to laugh. 'That is where our fat friends hang out. The Carbury sisters are apparently, beauticians from USA. The receptionist was quite forthcoming, until Miss Carbury appeared and then she virtually closed her down. I would have liked to have a chat to her away from here. We could ask in the village if she is a local girl. I can't chat her up, as I am Lady Frobisher and she will recognise me.

'Lady Frobisher?' Georgina was laughing. 'Oh Harriet, you are a nitwit!'

Harriet was deep in thought.

'That girl was scared of the Carbury woman. She certainly didn't like Letticia telling me who owned the clinic. I think, if Glenys was taken there, she would have been very scared. Whatever induced her to go and have her breasts enlarged?'

'She was in love with Bishop, remember? And if he told her he could get her a job as a model if she had bigger boobs, then she would probably have gone anywhere to please him.'

'We will have to try and ask Glenys, not sure how to do that without upsetting her and her mother.'

Georgina pulled into a lay-by, as she wanted to hear more about the Manor.

As they sat there, a cyclist came pedalling along the road. Harriet turned her head as the bicycle went past.

'That's the receptionist Letticia. Follow her slowly, don't let her see you, keep well back.'

Georgina pulled slowly out of the lay-by and waited till the cycle was nearly at the next bend and then followed. When the cyclist got to the village, she got off her bike and wheeled it up the path of a small cottage next to the village post office.

Georgina stopped the car a few yards up the road. 'What do we do now?'

'I will knock on the door and pretend that I was worried that she had got into trouble for saying too much about the clinic. That Carbury woman looked cross when she came down the stairs.'

'Was she one of the women we saw in the garden centre?'

Harriet nodded as she got out of the car.

She opened the gate to the cottage and went up to the front door and knocked on the door, with the highly polished horse shoe shaped brass knocker. The door was opened by a small woman, wearing a wraparound pinafore.

'Yes,' she said, looking suspiciously at Harriet.

'I am sorry to bother you, but I was worried about Letticia. I was up at the Manor and she was helping me with my enquiry regarding an appointment. I think her employer seemed cross at the attention Letticia was giving me, goodness only knows why. Is she alright?'

'That's kind of you, she is in a bit of a state. Perhaps you would like to come in.'

The woman stood back and Harriet stepped into the immaculate sitting room. The house smelled of lavender wax polish and everything gleamed. She followed the woman into an equally clean and tidy kitchen. Letticia was sitting at the table. It was obvious that she had been crying.

'Letty this lady was concerned that you got into trouble at the Manor.'

Letticia looked up and seemed very surprised to see Harriet.

'Lady Frobisher? Thank you for being worried. Yes, Miss Carbury had a real go at me. She told me I was only employed to give out brochures and make appointments, not to discuss private things about who owned the Manor. She told me to get my coat and not to bother coming back. She screamed at me and I was really scared of her, she has a terrible temper.'

'I am so sorry Letty; may I call you that?'

Letty nodded.

'I was not really interested in an appointment. I will be honest with you. I believe a friend of mine had treatment at the clinic and she had serious complications after the operation. I was trying to find out what goes on there and who does the operations and what is the involvement of the Carbury sisters. I am sorry that you got the sack because of me.'

Letty got up from the kitchen table.

'I am not to upset at getting the sack. I was thinking of leaving anyway. It was the way Miss Carbury spoke to me, that upset me.'

Letty went to a drawer in the kitchen dresser and took out a small book.

'I have kept a diary for the past few months as there have been some strange things happen. I have also heard the Carbury sisters arguing with various people. I think they are struggling for cash. I haven't been paid this month either.'

'I would be very happy to hear your story, Letty. My friend is outside in the car, would you mind if she came in and listened to your tale? As we are researching this thing together.'

The girl's mother said she would put the kettle on, while Harriet went to get Georgina.

Harriet went to the gate of the cottage and beckoned Georgie. She locked the car and trotted up to Harriet, who explained the situation.

'Poor Letty, I feel awful she has lost her job, but I get the impression that she is happy to leave the Manor.' Harriet told her friend and they went into the cottage, just as a large blue 4x4 drove slowly past.

'Think that was the vehicle that was parked outside the Manor. Hope they weren't going to come and give Letty more abuse!'

Letty's mother, who insisted they call her Iris, had made them all a cup of tea. They all settled down at the kitchen table.

'What do you want to know Lady Frobisher?'

'Well, for a start, you can call me Harriet and my friend here is Georgina. What started to make you suspicious at the Manor?'

'I started at the Manor about six months ago. I didn't have any experience as a receptionist. I was interviewed by the younger Miss Carbury, Fenella. After she had told me I had got the job, she left the room and I heard her talking to her sister, who asked why I had been given the job and Fenella said that she thought I was thick enough not to be a nuisance! I was a bit upset about that, but I took it thinking she was only joking and I had got the job.

'It was ok for a while, the patients that came for Botox were seen by Miss Celeste, Miss Fenella didn't do any procedures, she was more administrative. The operations like breast enhancements and tummy tucks were done by Dr Choudery.'

Letty started to leaf through her diary.

'At the beginning of August, there was a big argument between Miss Celeste and Mr Choudery, as he liked to be called. I was taking the post up to Miss Fenella's office, when I heard Miss Celeste shouting at him. It was something about which implants they were ordering. Mr Choudery was saying that the cheaper implants from the middle east were not stable. She was arguing about the price. Miss Fenella came out of her office, snatched the post from my hand and told me to go back downstairs, she went into the office where her sister and Mr Choudery were, and slammed the door shut.'

Harriet looked at Georgina.

'So perhaps they were using cheap, sub-standard implants?'

'Yes, that might have been why Glenys's op went wrong,' Georgina said thoughtfully.

'Do you mean Glenys Perry? She was here twice. Mr Choudery did her first operation, but he was gone by the time she came back.'

'Where did Mr Choudery go, and why?'

Letty looked through her diary again. 'He did Glenys's operation early in August, and Mr Choudery left at the end of August. I don't know why he left, I didn't even know he was leaving.

'I took a phone call from Mrs Perry to say something wasn't right with the implants on the twenty fourth of August. Afterwards that day, I heard Miss Celeste and Mr Choudery arguing, but I was sent home early that day by Miss Fenella.'

'So, what happened? Did Glenys get another appointment and come back for more treatment?' Georgina asked.

'I made an appointment for her on the first of September, but I wasn't there. Miss Fenella gave me the day off. She told me she wanted to look at the appointment books and would be sitting at my desk all day. I was pleased, cos it was my mum's birthday.'

'So, I assume Glenys Perry was still here the next day, if she was to have another operation. And who was going to do it if Choudery had gone?'

Letty looked confused. 'No Glenys wasn't here overnight and I don't know what happened to her notes. I did look for them. I usually file the patient's files from the day before, first thing in the morning. I didn't dare ask Miss Fenella.'

'Has Glenys been back here since?' Georgina asked.

'No, but Mrs Perry phoned on, let me see.' She looked at her diary again.

'Mrs Perry phoned two days after Glenys's appointment on the third of September, she asked to speak to Miss Carbury. I have no idea why she wanted to speak to her or what was said. She sounded agitated.

'Oh, wait a minute, I have put a note at the bottom of the page in my diary. 'Miss C went off in her 4x4 straight after the phone call from Mrs Perry.' Think she might have gone to see Glenys, but I don't really know.'

Harriet didn't think they could push Letty too much more.

'Well thank you, Letty. I would keep clear of the Carbury's, they don't seem to be the nicest of employers. I think it would be best, if you do not mention our conversation to anyone at the moment.'

'No, I won't say anything. I will go to the job centre tomorrow and sign on and look for another job.'

She was just closing her diary, when she stopped at a page.

'Oh, there was something odd that I wrote down in here on twenty-eight August. 'Muddy footprints all over reception.' I remember now. When I came to work, the front reception hall had muddy footprints leading up the stairs. Miss F was mopping the floor!'

Letty showed the diary entry to Harriet and Georgina.

'For Miss Fenella to be doing cleaning was so unusual, she usually wouldn't get her hands dirty. She told me that the cleaners hadn't turned up the evening before.

When I spoke to my friend who did the cleaning at that time, she said they had been as usual. The only thing I could think of, was that one of the workmen who was removing the old septic tank in the garden had wandered in after cleaners had been. But it was strange.'

Georgina and Harriet gave Lettie their mobile telephone numbers then thanked Iris for the cup of tea and left the cottage.

'You didn't correct Letty when she said 'goodbye Lady Frobisher'?' Georgina said, as they walked back to the car.

'No, it's better she doesn't know who we are. Harriet and Georgina is all she needs to know at the moment.

Both the women had a lot to think about.

They travelled back to Gorlstone in thoughtful silence.

Georgina dropped Harriet at the end of her road, 'I'll go and get my newspaper, if there is any news about the Johnson-Hargreaves, I will ring you.'

Harriet got out of the car, waved goodbye to her friend and went to the shop.

'Hello Harriet, come for your paper?' Penny Martindale said.

'Yes. How's things?'

'Have you heard what happened last night Harriet?'

'Last night? I had an early night, a long bath, nails and the rest, what did I miss?'

'Well someone in a car, threw a brick through Mrs Johnson-'Snotty Pants' BMW.'

Harriet looked shocked, 'Someone didn't like them then.'

'Old Jim heard it, but by the time he got out of his front door, they had driven off!'

'Couldn't have happened to a nicer person. No, I shouldn't say that I suppose, but at least their insurance will sort it out.'

'Then today she came over to say that the daughter's cat had escaped, but wasn't too bothered. She said that she expected the stupid thing had been run over by now. Apparently, the daughter was bored with the animal now anyway, and wanted some electronic toy, her friends have all got.

'But did ask us to keep an eye out for a, long-haired, white male cat, as the cat was valuable. Poor little bugger, bet he is as far away from here as he can get!'

Harriet got her paper and went home. She phoned Georgina and told her what Penny had said about the cat.

'Well, I haven't seen a white, long-haired male cat. I have seen a, short-haired, female, ginger pussy cat, that I am going adopt from an old lady who is going into a nursing home!' Georgina said innocently.

'Georgie, you haven't have you? So, the gravy browning worked but didn't know you did sex change ops as well.'

'Could you tell what sex a cat was by just looking at them? Especially if the vital bits have been removed? That's my story which I will tell Penny Martindale eventually, and I don't need to tell anyone else, she will do that for us!'

Harriet laughed and knew her friend would love having Dino to cuddle and she was sure Dino would enjoy being with Georgie.

The Accident

The next day, Harriet was about to cross the road on her way to Georgina, when she met Janice coming out of her gate. Janie was behind her and had a suitcase with her.

'Hi Janice, Janie. Are you off on holiday?'

Janice came closer to Harriet and said in a quiet voice, 'Janie is going up to Blackpool to find Nelson and Teddy. We are telling everyone else that she is going up to stay with my sister who is not well.'

Janie smiled and looked excited.

'I had a talk to Sheryl when I was in the pub with Tim yesterday, and she told me how her sister had seen Nelson and Teddy the night Jason was killed. So, it is obvious that Nelson had nothing to do with his death.'

Janice butted in, 'I am satisfied that Nelson didn't meet Jason, so I have given Janie the train fare to go and find the baby and Nelson. If they want to, I am happy for them all to come back here to live with me. I was a fool to have Jason here in the first place.'

Harriet was delighted. It was wrong for Janie to be apart from her baby. She knew Georgina would be very pleased.

She quickly took a note out of her bag and gave it to Janie, 'Buy the little man something from me, and it would be lovely if you all came back here in the village, but you do what will make you all happy.'

She gave the girl a hug and carried on over the road to Cherry Lane.

She tapped on Georgina's back door and opened the door and stepped inside. Laying in the basket by the Aga was a very happy ginger tabby cat, purring its head off as usual. When he saw Harriet, he stretched very leisurely, yawned and climbed out of the basket and strolled over to greet Harriet.

'Hello Dino, I love your new hairstyle,' she said giving him a stroke.

He or she as per her new persona, stuck her tail up in the air and went over to Georgina, jumped up onto her lap.

'Dino looks good, he seems to like being a ginger lady!'

Georgina got up and made coffee for them both. Harriet told her friend about Janie's trip to Blackpool, and that Janice had told her that, she, Nelson and Teddy would be welcome to come and live with her in Gorlstone.

'That's brilliant, she will have been missing that baby terribly. I am glad. Now where are we going with the murder problem? I have been thinking, we ought to try and talk to Glenys. How did she get the money for a boob job. The charges are extortionate, I have been looking at the price list Lettie gave you. '

A mobile phone started to ring, both women rushed to find the one that was ringing. It was Georgie's.

'Hello, oh hello Iris. Oh, my goodness, when did this happen?'

There was further conversation and Georgina ended the conversation and laid her phone down.

'Letty was knocked down this morning as she crossed the road to catch the bus to the job centre. Her mother says that only one person witnessed the accident and it was an old lady who has very poor eyesight. All she could tell the police was that it was a big car, possibly black or blue. Lettie has been taken to Palmouth hospital; she is still unconscious.'

'The blue 4x4 that was parked at the Manor passed us as we were going into Lettie's, could have been one of the Carbury sisters.'

'But you can't be sure it was them,' Georgina said. 'The vehicle would have dents or marks wouldn't it. We could go and have a look.'

'Look, I am the one who has the daft ideas, if the Carbury sisters can knock a young girl over then what chance would two old geriatrics have if they caught us!' Harriet said.

'Think we should go to the hospital and see Lettie. I don't think that it's not connected to Darrington Manor, I just have a feeling in my water.'

They settled Dino down with a cat treat and a cuddle, and went out and got into Georgina's car.

They got to the hospital and went in and asked which ward Lettie was in, then realised they didn't know her surname.

'She is the young woman who was in a road accident in Darrington, we were witnesses and concerned how the young woman is,' Harriet lied.

Just at that moment Georgina spied Iris in the hospital shop, 'Harriet there is Iris, Lettie's mother.'

Harriet and Georgina ran over to the shop and found Iris.

'How is Lettie, Iris?' Harriet asked the very worried looking woman.

'She has come round and is talking ok, but she has a broken leg. Come back to the ward with me and see her.' Iris told the two women.

'Did she see the car that hit her?' Harriet asked.

'She had her back to the car and it knocked her into the ditch, the impact knocked her out. She hit a wooden pole as she was thrown into the ditch. The pole has a big lump knocked out of it and the police think that the vehicle also hit the post.'

They reached the ward, Iris took them to the first bed, where Lettie was sitting up with a bandage round her head and her lower leg in plaster.

'Hello Lettie, how are you feeling love?' Georgina asked, as she took Lettie's hand.

'Not too bad, thank you for coming,' Lettie said.

Iris told them that the doctor had sent Lettie for a scan on the bump on her head but it had proved to be ok.

'The doctor said it was just a glancing blow to her head with the pole, it must have been the vehicle that really hit the wooden pole,' Iris told them.

'They want me to stay overnight, tonight, under observation and tomorrow if all is well, I can come home,' Lettie told her mother.

'That's good. You will have to rest up with that leg. Will they give you some crutches?' Iris asked her daughter.

'They will let me have a practice in the morning with the crutches. Apparently, it's not a bad break but I will have to keep the plaster on for about six weeks.'

They stayed and chatted to Lettie for a while. Harriet went back down to the shop and bought several magazines for Lettie, for which she was very pleased.

They left Iris with her daughter and made their way out of the ward.

Harriet saw one of the nurses at the nurses' station and went over to her.

'That young woman in the first bed, will you keep an eye on her? She was the victim of a hit and run accident. If anyone comes to see her, will you ask your colleagues to vet her visitors, as the perpetrators might try to visit her to try and intimidate her not to say anything.'

The nurse made a note on the pad in front of her, and said, 'The police have already asked us to monitor her visitors. We didn't worry about you two, as you came in with her mother and she told us you were Lady Frobisher.'

Harriet and Georgina smiled at the nurse, and hurriedly left the hospital.

On the way home they talked about the situation.

'My idea that someone should check the Darrington Manor 4x4 wasn't so silly you know,' Georgina said. 'But we can't do it, that would be stupid, but I have an idea.' She pulled the car over to a telephone box on the side of the road.

Georgina got out and found some coins in her purse. Harriet followed her into the phone box.

Georgina got out a piece of paper out of her bag. It had the police station's number on it that had been given to Janie when she was questioned about Jason. Janie had passed it on to Georgina.

She dialled the number and when the call was answered, Georgina spoke with a very suspect Scottish accent.

'Hey laddie take this doon, I will nae be repeating misself. Tell yon Inspector to check the blue 4x4 that is owned by the Carbury sisters who live in Darrington Manor, it was them that ran doon the lassie in Darrington this morning.'

Georgina slammed the receiver down and both women dashed out of the phone box.

'Just a minute,' Harriet said and ran back into the telephone box. She put her leather gloves on which she had in her pocket and wiped the receiver with her scarf and the door on both sides. She dived out of the phone box and ran to the car.

'Drive, Sherlock.'

Georgina put the car in gear and did a most unlike Georgina take off down the road.

'You wouldn't make a good criminal. The fuzz can trace phone calls and they could come to that box and look for fingerprints.' Harriet said, laughing at the horrified look on her friend's face.

'Oh Harriet, 'the fuzz', you sound like a criminal on tv!'

'Just being careful Sherlock! We want someone to go and look at the car that belongs to the Carbury sisters, and who better than the police. I wouldn't be at all surprised if they don't tell the police that their motor has been stolen!'

'That's what I would do if I had run someone over, well we will see what happens.'

The two women drove home in silence. It was nearly lunch time, so they decided to go into the Plough and have a light lunch. They found a table near the window and sat chatting.

'I think it's time we went and had a conversation with that Inspector in Palmouth, don't you?' Georgina said.

Just as the women were finishing the sandwiches they had ordered, old Jim came into the pub.

'Afternoon ladies, can I get you both a drink?'

'That's nice of you Jim, but we are having coffees.' Harriet told him.

'I will pay for the ladies' coffees; I will have a half of Guinness.' Jim pulled up a chair to their table and sat down. 'Have you seen the 'For Sale' sign up the road at the Gables?'

'No, when did that go up then? Wonder why they are selling up?' Georgina asked.

'Johnson-Hargreaves was in here the other night, and told me that they are moving to France. Bought an interest in a golf course out there. He was bragging as usual about it all. So good riddance is all I have to say.' Tom the landlord told them.

Georgina suddenly thought of Dino. If the Johnson-Hargreaves left the village and even the country, Dino would be safe.

'Suppose the incident of the brick through his BMW windscreen helped to make them feel not so loved!' Jim said with a twinkle in his eye.

'Very sad that, what an awful thing for someone to do!' Harriet said.

Tom laughed. Probably thinking that whoever had done it, deserved a medal.

Accidental Death or Not?

At Palmouth police station, Inspector Paul Kennedy sat at his desk. He had just reread all the statements concerning the murder of Jason Bishop.

It was now a few days after the murder and he was getting very frustrated and no further forward.

He called Sergeant Robbins into his office, 'Bring some coffee with you Clive, we need to try and get some sense out of all this.'

Sergeant Robbins brought the coffee and the two men sat down and looked through all the statements.

'I think we are missing something. I don't think we have been told the whole truth by several of these people,' Paul Kennedy said.

'I am wondering if that old biddy was quite as daft as I thought. She seemed to think that there were flowers at the crime scene. Why would she make that up? Think I had better go and have a chat with her. She was having a meal in the Park Hotel with the Robert's girl on Saturday,' Clive said, as he sipped his coffee.

'I got the impression that the Robert's girl didn't like Bishop at all, but I can't see her being able to attack him as he was a big lump of a bloke.'

'I just got a copy of the post-mortem. They reckon the wounds were inflicted by a long, pointed weapon, not a knife, more like a poker,' Paul said.

'Not many pokers laying around in the park, so someone must have brought the weapon with them,' Clive said laughing.

The Inspectors phone rang, 'Kennedy. Hi Doc... Well that's very interesting, are you hundred per cent sure about that? That could open up a real can of worms. Thanks, Mike.'

Paul grinned at Clive, 'What about this then? You remember the Streatham chap that was found dead in St Thomas's Street? The swabs they took from his body match Jason Bishop! They didn't find a match till Bishop's body was brought in.'

'Bloody hell! We wrote that off as an accident. He had a thin skull and the pathology report suggested at the time that Richard Streatham could have just tripped and hit his head on the wall. What's he saying now then?'

'Mike Ash is going to call the coroner's office as he wants reopen the case. He said at the time there were unexplained bruising to Streatham's face and he wasn't satisfied. The coroner had given an extension of time and was awaiting the results of the further tests.'

'The family were getting anxious that his body has not been released. But Mike Ash said he wasn't happy until he had done further tests and was awaiting results. Now he thinks Streatham was grabbed and probably slammed into the wall.'

'So, our friend Bishop has now been tied to this? Didn't the Streatham girl say that her step-father had spoken to Bishop and warned him off. What if Bishop took umbrage to this and attacked Streatham? The daughter knew that her step-father had warned him off.'

'Do we know where Bishop was on the night Streatham died? Perhaps Janice Roberts can help us on that. You go tomorrow to see her and then go on to find that old dear who mentioned the flowers. Do you know where she lives?'

Clive had to think, 'Think she must live near the Roberts woman, as she said she had seen me when I fetched Janice Roberts in to make her statement. I forgot to tell you, PC Baines followed up that anonymous phone call about the girl who was knocked down in Darrington. A Miss Carbury from the Darrington Manor rung up this morning to say that when they got up their 4x4 had been stolen!'

Inspector Kennedy raised his eyebrows, 'Humph that is convenient, what is that place? Some sort of spa or something? Do we know anything about this Carbury woman?'

'I will get WPC Wendy Jones to follow that up, seems like it needs a woman's touch!' Clive said.

'Well, we have now got a couple of questions we need answered. The men who were in the Plough seem to all have alibi's for the evening Bishop was killed, apart from the farmer in Gorlstone. Think we need to speak to him again. Bishop was not liked by anybody but we just don't seem to be able to find a link to his killer.'

At that moment, Paul's phone went again. Clive could tell from the Inspector's responses that something serious was afoot.

'We will have to delay our trip to Gorlstone. That was the Chief Super's office. The bank raids that have taken place in the south have now become our problem. They have had a tip off, that the Lloyds Bank at Chawton is to be hit in the next few days. Seems it's the same gang they have been watching. It's now a priority to catch these bastards. The last bank they hit one of the security guards was badly hurt and is still unconscious in hospital.'

'Oops looks like all leave is cancelled for a few days. There goes my golf day tomorrow!' Clive said, as he made his way to his own office to collect his kit and coat.

Glenys

Georgina and Harriet spent the morning on household chores. Harriet took her two dogs for a walk down Ashdown Lane, to the little stream at the bottom. The two dogs enjoyed splashing about in the water, retrieving sticks that Harriet threw for them.

When she got home, she made a sandwich and had a cup of tea. Her mind was going over the whole murder situation, the more she thought about it, the more she convinced herself that Darrington Manor was somehow involved.

After she had washed her lunchtime dishes, she put her coat on and was going to go over to Georgina's.

A knock came on her door and Georgina appeared through the kitchen door.

'I was just going to come over to you,' Harriet said.

'I haven't stopped thinking about Lettie and Darrington Manor. I am sure there is some connection but for the life of me I can't put my finger on it! We really need to speak to Glenys Perry. I am fed up with trying to sort it all out. I was going to suggest we forget it for a while. I would like to go to the garden centre to see if the bedding plants are in yet, want to come?'

'Good idea, let's go. We can have a coffee and a large piece of one of their scrumptious cakes. I will drive today.'

The weather was sunny for a change, with a little breeze. The garden centre wasn't very busy and some new plants had just come in. Georgina got a trolley and selected a few boxes of bedding plants.

'Hope we don't get a late frost. I will put them in the greenhouse for a few days, just in case.'

As she turned her trolley, she collided with another trolley. 'Oops so sorry. Oh, hello, Mrs Perry.'

Agnes Perry had several shrubs in her trolley and said, 'Looks as though the sun has made us all think of our gardens.'

Georgina had a sudden brainwave! 'Mrs Sharples told us that you have a lovely garden. I wish I knew more about plants and things. I don't suppose you would give me some advice. I buy plants and then don't know where I should plant them or how to look after them.'

Agnes loved gardening and was something of an expert where plants were concerned.

She liked to discuss her gardening ideas and, in the past, had often given talks to local gardening clubs. Since Glenys illness, she had not had the time to spare.

'I would be happy to advise you, I am sorry I can't remember your name and where you live.'

Georgina quickly said, 'I live in Cherry Lane in Gorlstone, I am Georgina Wright and my friend here is Harriet Holt.'

'Of course, I remember now. I can't do anything today, as Glenys has a doctor's appointment this afternoon.'

'How about you and Glenys come round tomorrow afternoon for tea and I can pick your brains about my garden. I would be so very grateful,' Georgina said eagerly, hoping she didn't sound too keen.

'That would be very nice,' Agnes said, 'We don't go out very much since Glenys has been poorly, but she seems to be getting better slowly. She has lost her confidence.'

'We will look forward to seeing you both tomorrow, Mrs Perry. I think this good weather is due to last for a day or two.'

They said their goodbyes and Harriet and Georgina went to the café and treated themselves to two huge lumps of Victoria sponge, both feeling very pleased with themselves.

'Seems as though we can't escape this mystery, can we Sherlock?' Harriet said laughing.

The following morning, both Harriet and Georgina did some baking for the impending tea party.

'I will take Agnes out into the garden and you can interrogate Glenys,' Georgina said, as they were laying the cakes and sandwiches out on plates in Georgina's kitchen.

'Interrogate? Make me sound like the MFI!'

'MI5. You dope,' Georgina said laughing.

'Sorry, I get my worms mixed up. Think I will approach the subject of her illness, very carefully.' Harriet could be subtle if she put her mind to it, which wasn't often!

A small blue car drove up Cherry Lane and parked outside Georgina's house at two. Glenys was driving.

Georgina went to her front door and stood waiting, while Agnes and Glenys Perry got out of their car, opened the gate and slowly walked up the path to Georgina's door.

'Welcome to my humble abode,' Georgina said.

'I see you have some nice strong hydrangeas in your front garden. You must have acidic soil for them to look so happy,' Agnes said, as she stepped inside the bungalow.

'Hello, Agnes,' Harriet said, coming out of the kitchen.

Suddenly Glenys caught sight of Dino, who had come to see who was coming into the house.

'Oh isn't he gorgeous, can I stroke him?' she asked.

'This is Dino and he is a girl, I mean she is a girl,' Georgina said, as Glenys got down on her knees and was being attacked by Dino's body, as he rubbed himself round her, purring, as usual, as loud as he could.

'She certainly seems to like you Glenys.'

'Will she let me pick her up?'

'I think that is what she is hoping, take a seat in the lounge, and I am sure she will join you for a cuddle.'

Glenys went and sat on the coach and Dino leapt straight onto her lap.

'Come and sit-down Agnes. Harriet, bring in the tea trolley. We will have our tea first.'

Harriet wheeled in the loaded tea trolley and started to pour out the cups of tea. She handed everyone a plate and then passed round the plate of sandwiches.

'These are delicious Harriet. I prefer Cos lettuce myself, rather than the popular Iceberg variety,' Agnes said.

Both Agnes and Glenys ate several sandwiches followed by a couple of pieces of the cakes that had been freshly made that morning.

'This is the most I have seen Glenys eat for some time,' her mother said.

'You don't make cakes as good as Mrs Wright, mother,' Glenys said smiling.

After they had finished eating, Georgina wheeled the trolley to one side and said, 'Shall we go and have a look at my back garden. I don't think Dino is going to like being disturbed, Glenys. So, you stay here and keep Harriet company.'

Georgina opened the French doors which led out to the garden and Agnes got up and followed her out into the garden.

Dino was still purring very loudly and shut her eyes and went to sleep on Glenys's lap.

'Your Mother told us you haven't been very well, I hope you are on the mend now,' Harriet said.

'Yes, thank you. It is the first time I have driven since um…my operation.'

'Do you know Lettie who lives in Darrington?' Glenys looked a bit panicky, so Harriet continued quickly.

'She was knocked down on Monday morning in the street at Darrington, had you heard?'

'My goodness, no I didn't know. Is she ok?' Glenys looked genuinely astonished.

'She has a broken leg and is probably home from hospital by now. Georgina and I feel it may have been our fault.'

'Why, did you run her over?'

'Good gracious, no!'

'Do you know Janie Roberts? We are special friends of Janie's. Georgina and I are trying to help her over a situation that has happened to her.'

'I saw Janie in the Park Hotel last Saturday with Tim. She confided in me as we used to be best friends. Things happened that we didn't agree on and I hadn't seen her for some time. Is it the baby thing, she did tell me, she was so worried. It was lovely to be friends again.'

'Was the thing you fell out over Jason Bishop?' Harriet asked.

Glenys burst into tears. 'I was so stupid, but I wouldn't listen to my friends.'

'Was it you who put the flowers on the park?'

'Oh God, did you see them? My mum followed me into Palmouth and removed them.'

'The police didn't see them, so you are ok. Can you tell me what happened between you and Jason if it's not too painful. There is a murderer out there somewhere and needs to be caught.'

Glenys looked thoughtful and seemed to make a decision.

'I met Jason in the Harbour Social Club. I was there with Sarah Davies, she works there now and calls herself, Serina. Her sister Sheryl works in the Park Hotel. She was with Jason. We used to like a dance. After hours when the old boss owned the place; they would lock the doors and we would have a bit of a party. Jason used to like watching us girls dance. He told me and Sarah that he could get us a job as professional dancers in London. That was always my dream. He told us that we would have to have bigger boobs for a London agent to be interested. Sarah told him to get lost, but she was bigger than me.

'He kept on about it and he started to take me out and he dropped Sarah. She wasn't too bothered as she told me that he had a terrible temper and had actually hit her. I didn't believe her then! Jason told me that Sarah's step-father had got funny with him over dropping Sarah, but he told me that he had put him in his place. Didn't know what he meant by that!

'I was besotted with Jason stupidly and he talked me into going to this clinic for an appointment to see about breast enhancement. It all sounded very simple and I read about the models in the paper having it done and they looked alright, so I agreed. Jason said he would pay for it as he said he wanted to be my agent. He said he would take the payment for the operation as a percentage of my earnings, once I got a job in London.

'I went to Darrington Manor and saw Sister Carbury and Dr Choudery. He was very nice; I was a bit scared of Sister Carbury though. The operation was done. I was a little sore but came home after two days. I hadn't told my mother about it. After three weeks, I began to see inflammation around the wounds and fluid seemed to be gathering around my breasts.

'My mother made me tell her what I had done. She rang the clinic and another appointment was made about a week later. My mother took me and she had words with Sister Carbury. Mother demanded to see the doctor, but Sister Carbury said wasn't possible. I didn't see him either. I was taken to theatre and that was the last thing I remember. When I came round, the implants had been removed and once I was conscious, I was allowed to go home. I felt terrible, but told to stay in bed and take some anti-biotics Sister Carbury gave me.

'Three days later I was in agony, mother phoned the clinic and Sister Carbury came out to the house. She gave my mother some money. She said it was compensation as the implants had failed. We didn't understand, she told us that she wouldn't pay the compensation if we told anyone who had done the operation, as it would be bad for the clinic. Apparently, she said that these things do happen. We were struggling to pay for the prescriptions she gave us for the anti-biotics, so we agreed to keep quiet.

'Then I got really ill and was admitted to hospital with toxic shock syndrome, caused by the infection. We told the hospital I had the operation abroad and they never queried it.'

'What did Jason say when he knew?' Harriet asked.

'He dropped me like a stone. Didn't even come to see me.'

Harriet thought to herself that the world was a better place without Jason Bishop.

'Georgina and I went to the Darrington Clinic to see what we could find out. Lettie was telling me about Miss Carbury, but she overheard the conversation. Poor Lettie was sacked after we left. Then she was knocked over the next day by a hit and run driver. We wondered if the Carbury's were afraid of what Lettie might tell someone. We have told the police to go and check on the Carbury's vehicle.'

'It was strange that I never saw Dr Choudery at all on the second visit. He was so attentive when I had the implants put in. He did actually try and persuade me not to have the implants when Sister Carbury was out of the room, on the first visit, which I thought strange.'

At that moment, Agnes and Georgina came in from the garden. Glenys stopped talking and shook her head at Harriet and put her finger to her lips. Harriet got the message and changed the subject.

'Your daughter has fallen in love with Dino, Agnes.'

'I was thinking of getting another cat, perhaps a kitten would be fun, what do you think Glenys?' Agnes said.

'Your mother told me a little about your illness Glenys, I hope you don't mind. Jason Bishop was a bad lot, but someone has killed him so I feel we must be careful who we all talk to about the whole situation,' Georgina said quietly. 'Now shall we have another cup of tea and a piece of Harriet's Apple cake, I will warm it up and we will have some cream with it.' Georgina left the room to cut the pieces of cake.

'I think that would be wise not to discuss all this. I have a feeling there is more to be uncovered by the police. And I think a kitten would be a wonderful idea. I know Joe Clarke's cat gave birth a few weeks ago. I can give him a ring to see if he still has the kittens,' Harriet said.

'That would be a good idea, Harriet,' Agnes said.

Harriet dialled Joe's number. Harriet explained she was enquiring about the kittens and told Joe who was interested. Joe said that he still had two kittens that he wanted good homes for. 'I am going to keep two of the kittens as they are good hunters and need to keep the mice under control.'

Georgina came back with the trolley, with four plates of heated apple cake and a jug of double cream.

'Wow,' Agnes said. 'We are really being spoiled today.'

Just then, Georgina's front door bell went, and she went to see who was at the door. She came back into the lounge followed by Joe. He had a box under his arm. He went over to Glenys and pulled back the blanket which was covering the top of the box. Two little heads popped up. The cutest of kittens.

Glenys eyes filled with tears, 'Mum just look at these, please can we have one?'

Agnes hadn't seen happiness in her daughter's eyes for many weeks, what could she say.

'Joe they are gorgeous, how much do you want for a kitten?'

'Agnes I can see they would have a good home; you can have them both as a gift. You were very kind when my mother died, and they would be good company for each other. What do you think?'

Agnes looked at Glenys who had a kitten under each arm, her face was radiant!

'I think we have just adopted two babies, is that ok with you Glenys? Thank you, Joe.'

Dino walked into the lounge, took one look at the kittens turned round with his tail in the air and went back into the kitchen. Georgina followed him and picked him up and gave him a cuddle and he settled down into his basket, purring as usual.

Joe left happy that the kittens had found a good home. Soon after, Glenys and Agnes left. They had all hoped the police would soon sort out the Jason affair. Georgina had told them that the police may need to know about the clinic and Jason Bishop's involvement, but agreed not to discuss anything other than with the police, and be careful not to aggravate the Carbury sisters. They had all decided that the Carbury sisters could have something to hide.

After their visitors had left, Harriet told Georgina the content of her conversation with Glenys. Georgina said that Agnes had actually brought up the subject of Jason Bishop.

'It was as though she needed to unload her thoughts.' She had told Georgina that she had several unsatisfactory conversations with both of the Carbury sisters. She said that she wouldn't have allowed Glenys to return to the clinic the second time, but Celeste Carbury had convinced her that the problem would be put right at no cost to Glenys or her mother, and was something that sometimes happened, the removal of the implants, and a course of anti-biotics would soon sort it all out.

'The Carbury woman definitely didn't want Glenys to go to her GP. I wonder if the implants were the cheap ones that Lettie said Dr Choudery objected to, and why did Choudery leave the clinic and when?'

'I think it's time we went and had a chat with that handsome police Inspector. If it was one of the Carbury's who ran Lettie down, then we don't want to be the next road kill,' Georgina said.

'Will he listen to us though? His Sergeant thought you were potty when you mentioned the flowers. Policemen don't like amateur snoops!'

Harriet nodded, 'We will just have to risk it, we will do it tomorrow.'

Wasted Journey

The following morning, Georgina as usual, was dressed smartly in a blue trouser suit. Harriet had gone through her wardrobe thinking that as the police probably thought, she was a batty old woman, she would dress in a more conservative fashion. She tried several ensembles and ended up finding a pair of black trousers, that she hadn't worn since Georgina's husband's funeral. She thought that a white blouse and a black jacket would finish off the look she was trying to achieve. The first white blouse she found had a hole nibbled in one sleeve, that Timmy her Jack Russel had decided he liked. The second blouse was cream but respectable, so she decided on abandoning the black and white theme.

Her usual pony tail was a pinned up in a French pleat. Harriet had a last look in the mirror and then realised she had to find shoes that matched. Wellies? No not today, so she found a pair of black ankle boots that desperately needed a polish. The finished Harriet looked very un-Harriet like, but she was satisfied that the figure she was trying to project was as near to her idea as it was possible.

When Harriet arrived at Georgina's door, she did feel very self-conscious.

'Blimey, who is this woman on my door step. Not a Jehovah's Witness!' Georgina said laughing. 'I know you fancied that Inspector Harry, suppose you have sprayed yourself with 'a come and get me' perfume!'

Harriet pulled a face, feeling decidedly uncomfortable, she really missed her baggy clothes.

'Let me just give Dino his breakfast, then we will go.'

They got into Georgina's car and made their way to Palmouth.

They talked about what they were going to tell the police. It was agreed that no mention of Nelson was going to be made. As far as anyone was concerned, Janie had gone up north to stay with her aunt Helen.

When they arrived at the police station, they parked as near as it was possible. There was no public parking outside the station, but fortunately they found a spot in a side road very near.

'What is that Inspector's name? Can you remember Harriet?'

'Think it was Paul something. I remember thinking of Paul Newman, but not sure what his surname is.'

'Stop dribbling Harriet, hope you are going to be able to think straight instead of gazing at him!'

Harriet laughed, 'I think it's important that he takes us serious, so no I won't dribble.'

The desk Sergeant smiled at the two ladies. He immediately thought they had come to report a lost cat or something similar.

'Good morning, Sergeant,' Georgina said. 'We want to speak to the Inspector who is dealing with the Jason Bishop murder.'

'I am sorry ladies; Inspector Kennedy is out of the station for a few days. WPC Wendy Jones is dealing with the case in the Inspector's absence, she can deal with any information you may have. I will give her a call.'

'No, sorry Sergeant, we can only speak to the Inspector and it is a matter of some urgency. Also, we wondered if you had found the vehicle that ran down the young woman in Darrington?' Harriet wasn't going to be fobbed off.

'I cannot discuss a case, ladies, I am sorry.' The Sergeant started to move papers around on his desk as though the interview was over.

'I suppose the vehicle that hit her was stolen. That's an easy get out!' Harriet wasn't going to just walk away.

The Sergeant decided that he had better take some details from these two persistent 'old dears'.

He was experienced enough to know that these 'old dears' as he thought of them, sometimes gave useful information. They seemed to observe situations, not always put the right conclusions to things that happened, but occasionally hit the nail on the head.

'Right ladies can I take your names and addresses. I will then pass them on to Inspector Kennedy. He and his team have been seconded to another case, but as I understand it that case may have resolved itself last night, so the Inspector may be back later today or tomorrow. You said the information you have is related to the Bishop murder?'

'That is correct Sergeant,' Georgina said, a bit disappointed. Having both been primed to tell all, or nearly all to the police, they left a little dejected.

'Oh well, we will have to come back late tomorrow afternoon,' Harriet said.

They went and did some shopping in Palmouth before returning to Gorlstone.

Behind Closed Doors

Georgina spent the rest of the morning in her garden.

Harriet delightedly stripped off her smart clothes and was soon happily tugging on jeans and a large baggy t-shirt. She took Timmy and Snoopy for a long walk down the lane to the stream, where they happily splashed about getting very muddy.

On the way back up the lane, the subject of Darrington Manor was on her mind.

Over in Cherry Lane, Georgina's thoughts were on the same subject. She went to her handbag and found the leaflet that she had taken from the notice board at the Garden Centre.

'Aromatherapy Massage, I do like an aromatherapy massage,' she said to the cat. She put her coat on, then took it off again.

She then went to her telephone and dialled the number on the leaflet.

'Good morning, Darrington Manor Clinic, how can I help you?' Georgina recognised the voice, as one of the women, Harriet and she had seen at the garden centre.

'Good morning. I am interested in an aromatherapy massage as advertised in your leaflet,' Georgina said.

'Just a minute, I will put you through to Margery, our aromatherapist,' the woman said.

'Thank you.' Georgina wasn't going to back down now.

The phone was picked up by presumably Margery.

Georgina enquired the availability and the price of an aromatherapy massage and was offered an appointment that very afternoon. Margery told her that she had an appointment free, as another client had just cancelled.

Georgina gave her name as Fletcher, which was actually her maiden name. She disguised her phone number by adding the code for her number, not to be recorded by the recipient.

'Thank you very much. I really need a relaxing massage; life has been a little stressful lately'

Margery sounded really pleasant, 'I will look forward to meeting you Mrs Fletcher, at two-thirty.'

Georgina thought, 'This cloak and dagger thing is catching on to me. It's usually Harriet that does dopey things. I will run over and tell her.'

By the time she arrived at Harriet's, Georgina was beginning to doubt her sanity. When she told Harriet, she laughed and voiced exactly what Georgina had been thinking, 'I am the mad bitch that has crazy ideas, not you Georgie. You will have to drive my car, as it was your car that we went to Darrington Manor in before.'

Georgina had driven Harriet's car before, so that would not be a problem.

'Yes, you are right Sherlock, glad your brain is working.'

'Now, take your mobile with you, and be careful, if the Carbury's are up to something, they won't want anyone poking around. You might get some information from the aromatherapist, but remember she could get suspicious if you ask too many questions. I will drive to Darrington in your car and go and see Iris, so I won't be too far away.'

'Ok, thanks.'

Georgina went back home taking Harriet's car. She went inside to get ready for her treatment. She left at about one, after Harriet came over to collect her car. In her rear mirror she caught sight of Harriet following her, and saw her pull over and park outside Iris's house in Darrington village.

On arriving outside Darrington Manor, Georgina parked Harriet's car in the lay-by on the main road. As she wanted to walk up the drive. She walked up the stone steps to the front door. After she had rung the bell, the door was opened by the younger Miss Carbury.

They obviously had not replaced Letticia.

'Good afternoon. I have an appointment for an aromatherapy treatment,' Georgina said.

She had worn a large woollen beret style hat, that covered most of her hair. She had also raked out an old pair of horn-rimmed glasses, that she had kept of her husbands. When she had looked at herself in the mirror before she had left home, she thought the two things had changed her appearance enough she hoped that the Carbury sisters would not recognise her from the garden centre incident.

Miss Carbury led the way up the impressive staircase. At the top, she turned right and took Georgina around a gallery style corridor.

She had noticed two doors at the stop of the stairs that had notices on, stating the rooms were offices.

Miss Carbury indicated a door that was labelled 'The Aromatherapy Suite.'

'Here we are. Go inside and take a seat and Margery will be with you shortly.'

Georgina went in and found a pleasant room furnished with comfortable armchairs. There were magazines on a small oak coffee table. The room smelled sweetly of a mixture of lavender oil and another unknown scent, but very pleasant and welcoming.

The room Georgina was in, looked out over the gardens on the side of the old manor house. She had a look out of the window and could see a large area where obviously some alterations had been made, as an area of new grass was attempting to establish itself.

A door on the right-hand side of the reception room opened and a young black woman came in.

'Mrs Fletcher, how nice to meet you. Please come into the treatment room.'

Georgina followed the young woman. She was given a white towelling robe and a large white bath towel.

'If you will undress behind the screen and wrap the towel around you and put on the robe. Then return to this chair so that I can take some details.'

Georgina obeyed the instructions and emerged wrapped, as requested. She came and sat in the padded chair in front of the desk, where Margery was sitting pen poised with a form in front of her.

'Just a few questions for my file and to be sure you have no medical problems that I should be aware of.'

After telling Margery her name, Rebecca Fletcher, and an address, which Georgina had made up using names of roads that she knew existed in Palmouth, and her date of birth which she only altered slightly. There were a few questions about illnesses, current medication and general fitness.

'Are some people not able to have aromatherapy then,' Georgina asked.

'If you are having cancer treatment, aromatherapy is not advisable. But in the main event a very gentle massage can be beneficial to anyone with back pain and stress related problems. I would give a head and neck massage in some cases, but you sound in good health Mrs Fletcher. You said you would like a full body massage, which I am sure you will enjoy. Now please come with me to the couch and make yourself comfortable.'

Georgina was asked to lay face down on the treatment table. There was a hole where she could place her face, allowing her to lie flat. It did mean that it was not possible to speak to Margery while her back was being massaged.

The treatment was very professionally carried out and Georgina began to really enjoy the experience. Margery had switched on some very relaxing quiet music. She began to feel quite drowsy.

It was soon time to turn over for her ribs and stomach to receive the treatment. A towel was discreetly placed over her breasts and another over her pubic region. The arm massage was relaxing and the leg and stomach massage pleasant.

'What oils are you using Margery,' Georgina asked.

'Lavender, rose and a little sandalwood. The carrier oil is Calendula oil, as your skin was a little dry in places.'

'It is lovely. Would it be possible to buy some of that mixture to use at home?'

'Yes of course, I will mix you some to take home with you. Now I want you to relax for about twenty minutes, here on the couch. How do you feel now?'

'Wonderful, thank you Margery. I was very tense, now I feel really relaxed. How long have you worked here at the Manor?'

'For about seven months. I was working in Birmingham before.'

'Oh, so you must have known Dr Choudery then?'

Margery hesitated, 'You knew Mr Choudery then Mrs Fletcher?'

'Only through a friend who had implants. She said he was a very nice man.'

Margery got up from her chair and said, 'I will go and mix the oils for you to take home with you.'

'Oops, I seem to have hit a nerve,' Georgina thought.

A few minutes later, Margery returned with a bottle of ready mixed oils.

'I haven't given you a lot,' she said. 'As you only need a few drops. I suggest you concentrate on your legs, as the skin on your legs is quite dry. This will be very beneficial.'

Georgina was helped from the massage couch and she went behind the screen to get dressed.

'The lady that let me in is she the receptionist or is she a therapist?'

'That was Miss Fenella Carbury, the joint owner of the clinic. Why did you want to make another appointment?' Margery asked guardedly.

Georgina thought she had better say yes, as she realised she was asking too many questions.

'Yes, I would Margery, do I make it with you or Miss Carbury?'

Margery looked relieved, 'I can do that for you, when would you like to come next?'

'I have visitors coming next week, so can I make it the following week?'

Margery got out a diary and they arranged a time and date, which of course, Georgina had no intention of keeping. She paid for her massage and Margery showed her out.

'Is there a toilet I could use before I go?' She asked.

Margery pointed to a door next to the door marked 'office'.

'Thank you, Margery. I have enjoyed my massage I will recommend your services.'

The girl beamed; she was going to wait to show Georgina out, but she heard her phone begin to ring in her room.

Georgina waited till she heard Margery on the phone and she came back out of the toilets. She tapped on the office door and when no-one answered, she slipped inside. She quickly looked around and saw a large, walk-in cupboard with a bunch of keys hanging on the door. She went in and saw a man's overcoat rolled up on the floor over the top of a leather Gladstone bag. The bag had the initials K. I. C. printed on the side. Georgina undid the bag and found it full of medical equipment, obviously a doctor's bag.

'How strange,' she thought. If Dr Choudery had gone, what was his bag doing still here at the Manor.

At that moment she heard someone enter the office.

'For goodness's sake Fenella, you have left the bloody door unlocked. Anyone could have walked in.'

With that, the door was slammed shut and Georgina heard the key turn in the lock.

A very unladylike word came into Georgina's mind.

'I wonder if my phone works in a cupboard?' she thought. She looked around and realised that what she thought was a cupboard, was in fact part of the office that had been partitioned off to make this walk-in depository. At the far end, behind a pile of boxes, she found there was a window. She peered through the very grubby glass and saw that the ground was a long way down, not a chance of escaping out of the window, even if she could open it.

She couldn't hear any noise from the office, but then she heard voices. Georgina went to the pile of boxes by the window and climbed behind them and squatted down, just as the door was opened. Georgina was afraid to breathe.

'We will have to get rid of his things at the weekend. I will take the overcoat and throw it on the bonfire that gardener has started. I will wait until he has gone home. The bag will have to be disposed of. I did think it could go down the old well. What do you think Celeste?'

'I dealt with Bishop, didn't I? When he tried to blackmail us. The bastard! When I asked him for the money to pay for the Perry girl's op, he had the audacity to say he had paid that debt when he helped us to send the doc on his way!'

'Alright Celeste, don't keep on about it!'

'Just get on and do it. The gardener has just driven out and Margery has gone home. I will go and open a bottle of wine and hurry up. The quicker it's all done the better. I have booked our flights for next Tuesday and this place can go to hell, as far I am concerned.'

The cupboard door closed and Georgina heard the key turn once again.

Then she heard the outer office door closed, and once again, she heard the lock click into place.

Meanwhile, Harriet was getting anxious. She had several cups of tea with Iris and filled herself up with nearly half of one of Iris's amazing cakes.

Lettie had returned home after having been for an interview in a local dog kennels. The kennels were owned by old Jim Talbot's son and daughter-in-law. Jim had been visiting his son and had offered to give Lettie a lift home, as she had walked to the kennel, mainly to see if walking to work would be an option if she got the job.

Iris had invited Jim in for a cup of tea and he had enjoyed polishing off the rest of the cake that Harriet had been munching.

Harriet was becoming anxious and asked her how long an aromatherapy session should take.

'About an hour at the most. What time was her appointment?' Lettie asked.

'Two thirty. I hope she hasn't got into trouble. I am beginning to worry.' Harriet said. The time was now nearing four thirty.

'Well, if we don't hear anything by five, we will have to do something.' Harriet knew that Georgina would know that she would worry.

Ten minutes later, Harriet's phone rang.

'Georgie, are you all right?'

'Listen Harry, my battery is not going to last long. I am locked in a small room off of the main office on the west side of the Manor. Both the door to the small room and the main office has been locked. The only way out is a window on the first floor, if I can get the window open.'

Harriet gasped, 'Ok Sherlock, I am on the way, how will we know which window, we will have to get a ladder from somewhere.'

'There is a long ladder leaning against the old building I can see from this window. I will shine a light with my phone if I see you. But wait till it gets dark. The Miss Carbury's seem to live at the other end of the manor. I saw doors marked Private on the west side, so I assume that's their living quarters.'

Harriet had turned very pale. 'What's up love?' Jim asked.

Harriet told Jim, Iris and Lettie. They were horrified.

'How the hell did she get locked in?' Iris asked.

'I don't know, but she says the only way out is from the window. There is a long ladder apparently leaning against an old building on the east side,' Harriet said, feeling a little helpless.

'I know the Manor and know what building she means. Also, I have been in the office at the manor and think I know which room she is locked in, so the three musketeers have to reband my dear.' The old man had that gleam in his eyes that was there the night of the cat-nap.

'Hang on a minute,' Lettie said. 'Tonight is the night of the four musketeers. You don't think I am not going to help, do you?'

'Mum, you can man the phone. If we get into trouble, you can be the fifth musketeer. We will ring if we need help, ok?'

The light was beginning to fade, so the gang of desperados prepared for their task. They had black balaclavas which Jim found in his car. Harriet made no comment, but of course she knew their history and Iris found some gloves for both the women and gave them two small torches. It was decided that they would drive up to the lay-by near the entrance to the Manor in Georgina's car. Jim's Morris Minor was not considered to be an ideal get-away vehicle if things got hectic!

Iris was anxious but happy that Jim was with the two women.

Once it was dark, they got into the car and drove just past the entrance to the Manor and she parked in the lay-by, behind Harriet's car.

They crept up the driveway, treading on the grass. 'There is a security light that is pointing down the drive, so if we keep to the grass on the right-hand side, we shouldn't set it off,' Jim said quietly.

'I have just thought Jim, Georgina wore a slim line long skirt, how is she going to get out of the window?'

Jim grinned to himself, 'Looks like she will have to come down the ladder in her knickers.'

'Oh Jim, you are naughty,' Lettie whispered laughing.

They crossed the grass to the old building and soon located the ladder. Harriet looked up at the house and quickly switched her phone on and off. An answering light showed from the third window along on the first floor.

They carefully took the ladder down to a horizontal position and between them, they carried it over to the house.

Meanwhile, inside, Georgina had removed the boxes from the window and had tried to move the latch on the sash window. It obviously had not been opened for many years. I just wouldn't budge. Panic was setting in, so she looked around to try and find something to lever the catch loose with. The battery on her phone was fading fast and she was afraid that she wouldn't have enough light to signal Harriet.

She knocked over a bottle of something as she groped about for a lever. She sniffed and thought she recognised the smell. She put her finger down to the floor where the bottle had dropped being careful not to tread in whatever it was. She sniffed her fingers and realised it must be olive oil. She got a tissue out of her bag which she was still clutching, soaked it with the oil and then rubbed it all round the catch.

With a little shove the catch slid open. She then tried to raise the sash window, it moved slightly, then with an extra shove it moved upwards.

Then the skirt situation struck her, as it had Harriet. There was no way she could climb up onto the window ledge with the restriction of her skirt. She saw movements out in the garden and a flash of light which showed Harriet's worried face. Georgina turned her waning phone on but got just enough to show a glimmer.

The next thing the ladder appeared at the window. She heard someone climbing up, and then Lettie's face appeared.

'Hi Mrs Wright, fancy meeting you here,' she whispered.

'Lettie I am going to have to take my skirt off, can you take my handbag down with you. I will throw my skirt down, ok?'

Lettie climbed back down with Georgina's bag and a very surprised Jim suddenly found himself enveloped in the skirt as it flew down from the window above.

Georgina had fortunately put on a pair of leggings under her skirt, so although Jim as a gentleman, looked the other way, nothing too embarrassing was on show, as she slithered down the ladder.

They quickly replaced the ladder. Georgina had pulled the sash window down before she had descended the ladder, hoping that no-one would know anything untoward had taken place.

They all scampered as quietly as possible down the drive, and ran up the road to Georgina's car. As they got into the two cars. Jim offered to drive Harriet's car back to Iris's house.

'By Gum girls, life is not boring since I have known you two!' Jim said, as he got into the car. Obviously again thoroughly enjoyed the whole evening.

'Why, what other adventures have you three had then?' Lettie asked.

'We will tell you one day Lettie. Perhaps we will write a book.' Harriet told her.

When they got back to Iris's house, she was so relieved to see them all safe and sound.

Georgina had wriggled back into her skirt as she had sat in the back of the car, but Harriet made them all laugh in Iris's kitchen, as she showed the pictures she had taken of Georgina as she had descended down the ladder.

'I think these would go virol on the internet,' said Lettie.

'Oh no I will keep these in case Georgina misbehaves, as blackmail,' laughed Harriet.

'I think I cut a fine figure of a woman in my underwear, sliding down the ladder!' Georgina said.

'Lettie. Do you know what Dr Choudery's Christian name was?'

Lettie had to think for a minute, 'Yes, it was Kalid Idris Choudery, why?'

'Just wondering, that's all.'

Iris had a large pot of beef stew on her range and invited them all to have some.

'What a nice way to end a traumatic day,' Georgina said tucking in.

She couldn't wait to tell Harriet everything she had seen and heard. To explain her predicament of getting locked in, she told Iris, Jim and Lettie that she had mistaken the cupboard for the toilet and had been locked in before she realised her mistake.

Jim knowing the lay out of the building said nothing, but didn't believe a word of it. He thought to himself that possibly there was another adventure looming, so he kept quiet.

They said goodbye to Lettie and Iris, and thanked them for the help and refreshments. Jim left also and as he got in his car, he asked Georgina if he could come round and see the cat the following day, which of course she was happy about. Both the women liked Jim and were glad they had made such a good friend.

They drove their own cars back to Gorlstone and were both looking forward to get back to their prospective homes to put their feet up.

Georgina told Harriet all that she had discovered at the Manor when they got back to Gorlstone, which only confirmed their suspicions that the Carbury sisters had some questions to answer. They agreed to visit the police station the following day.

The Inspector Calls

The next day, the woman thought they would delay their visit to the police station till late afternoon to be sure that the Inspector would have returned to Palmouth. After the adventure of the previous day, Georgina decided to have a lie in. She was still in her pyjamas when Harriet appeared.

Harriet had tied her hair up in a chiffon scarf and had on her old gardening clothes. She had taken the dogs to the river earlier and had mud splashed on her anorak. She put the kettle on and made Georgina another cup of tea and one for herself.

They had just started to discuss the happenings at Darrington Manor, when the front door bell rang.

'It's probably old Jim, go and let him in Harriet, I'll go and put my clothes on.' Dino was still laying on Georgina's bed and when she came in, he stretched and demanded a cuddle.

Harriet opened the front door and was dismayed to see Inspector Kennedy and Sergeant Robbins standing on the doorstep.

'Good morning, Mrs Wright?' He said.

'No, I am Mrs Holt. Mrs Wright is indoors.' She nearly said, 'getting dressed' then thought twice before she said it.

'We can kill two birds with one stone then, as we would like to speak to you as well. I understand that you both came to the police station yesterday.'

'Yes, Inspector we were going to come back later today.'

She stood back and allowed the two officers to enter the bungalow. She took them into the lounge and then offered them a cup of tea, which they refused.

'I will call Georgina,' but at that moment she appeared hastily dressed.

'Good morning, Inspector. It is time that we should talk.' Georgina could be a little officious when she liked, and this morning she liked. Being taken unawares always annoyed her, so she wasn't in the mood to dither.

'Mrs Holt mentioned something to your Sergeant here,' she pointed at Sergeant Robbins. Harriet thought she was going to actually poke the younger policeman, 'But he made her feel she was a dithering old idiot who didn't know what she was talking about.'

The Inspector tried to get a word in, but Georgina was riled.

'We may be a little older than you, but we have all our marbles. So please I would appreciate it if you will sit and listen while we try to help you solve a case, which appears to be flummoxing you.'

Paul Kennedy wanted to smile but was afraid that if he did, Georgina might smack him and the Sergeant. It felt a bit like being in the headmistress's study, so he shut up!

'Humour the old dear' Sergeant Robbins thought.

'Now, for a start, there are many people who disliked Jason Bishop. We have some evidence that along with the few bits you have we can unravel this.

'Jason was going out with a girl called Glenys Perry. He persuaded her to have breast implants at the Darrington Manor Clinic. Which according to Glenys, Jason Bishop said he would pay for.

'These implants were done by a Dr Choudery. The implants for some reason failed and caused the girl to be ill. We know that prior to Glenys operation, Dr Choudery had a row with the owners of the clinic about the quality of the implants. He thought they were unreliable and this proved to be the case with Glenys. Her mother took her back to the clinic and the implants were removed, but we do not know who performed this operation, as according to our witness Dr Choudery had left the clinic or disappeared.

'Glenys was sent home the same day, as the removal was performed and subsequently became very ill. This can be proved by the hospital records. The Perry's were paid by the clinic, and pressured from Bishop not to tell the hospital, who had performed the operations. As they were struggling to pay for the antibiotics Glenys needed, they took the money and told the hospital that the operation had been done abroad.'

'How does all this connect with Bishop's murder?' Sergeant Robbins asked.

Harriet sat down next to Georgina.

'I went to the clinic pretended I was going to make an appointment for a procedure.'

The Inspector looked at Harriet, 'I wouldn't have thought you would need any improvement.'

Harriet blushed, 'Thank you kind sir. No, I was only trying to find out something about the place.

'Letticia Watson, the girl who was run down in Darrington was working there as the receptionist, a very helpful girl. She was answering my questions when Miss Carbury came down the stairs and it was obvious that she was angry that Letticia was talking to me. I actually beat a hasty retreat as we had an earlier problem with the Carbury sisters and I was hoping that she wouldn't recognise me.

'The Carbury woman sacked Lettie as soon as I left. We saw her cycling home and we followed her as we wanted to ask her some more questions. It was she, that told us that Choudery had suddenly disappeared from the Clinic.'

Harriet also told the policemen about Lettie finding the younger sister cleaning the mud from the hall and stairway. 'This was about the time that Dr Choudery disappeared. We don't want to be melodramatic, but it made us wonder. We understood that the Manor was having an old cesspool removed around that time and a new one fitted.'

'One thing that equates with that is that Bishop only worked on the building site in Palmouth for just over a month, before that he worked for M.C. Jones who service cess pits.' The Inspector told them.

Harriet thought that at least the police had got something useful to add to the pot.

'So, I don't see what this is leading to,' Paul Kennedy said.

Georgina took over the conversation.

'Yesterday, I made an appointment at the clinic for an aromatherapy massage. Harriet couldn't go, as they had already seen her and been suspicious. I had the massage and after asked if I could use the toilet. Fortunately, the phone rang and the aromatherapist left me to make my own way out of the Manor.'

Georgina related the story of how she got locked in and finding the doctors bag with his initials on and the over coat.

Clive Robbins laughed and said, 'I think these ladies read too many books sir.'

Georgina stood up and loomed over the Sergeant, 'Harriet, give me your phone.'

She took the phone and put on the video of the escape through the window. 'Now do you believe me?'

She then repeated the conversation that the two sisters had regarding Bishop and the doctor.

Inspector Kennedy was amazed. The video of Georgina coming down the ladder in her long johns had convinced him that there was some credence to the story and it was a sight that would linger long in both the policemen's minds for some time…

'Sergeant Robbins please take a statement from Mrs Wright and Mrs Holt; it appears we have been talking to the wrong people. I think it's time we paid a visit to Darrington Manor. One piece of information that aligns with what you have told us is, that Bishop only worked on the building site in Palmouth for about three to four weeks.'

Georgina related the content of the conversation she had heard, plus the other facts they had uncovered.

Sergeant Robbins reluctantly had to agree that the ladies had some interesting tales to tell. He got out his note book and was about to take down a statement from Georgina and Harriet, when the front door bell went. Harriet being nearest to the door went and found Jim on the doorstep.

'Hello, Jim, come in we have the police here. Think they are at last taking us seriously at last.'

Jim had advised them to speak to the police the evening before.

'Good morning, Mrs Wright.' He nodded at the Inspector and the Sergeant.

The Inspector got up and shook Jim's hand.

'Morning Jim, you know these ladies then,' he said.

'Know them lad? I was with them last night, they virtually solved this for you.' Jim was laughing.

The Inspector looked sheepish. 'Mr Talbot, or should I say ex-Chief Inspector Tate of Palmouth, retired for nearly ten years now, Jim, isn't it. Highly respected officer and we all owe a lot to Jim. You won't remember him Clive, but this man was a legend. Hope you are not getting into mischief; I did wonder when that cat went missing next door to you.'

Georgina held her breath and prayed that Dino would stay curled up on her bed.

The statements were taken and the police officers left. They needed to get a search warrant for Darrington Manor, as it was clear that the Carbury sisters had some questions to answer.

Jim stayed and had a cup of tea and was reintroduced to Dino.

'There's no need to worry about the Johnson-Hargreaves, there was a removal lorry outside early this morning and they have gone. The brat, according to Penny Martindale, has been sent to a boarding school where she will hopefully learn some manners.'

Georgina sighed with relief, 'I can let Dino's fur grow again then.'

'We will now hope the Inspector finds the answers to this case at Darrington Manor.'

Discoveries at the Manor

Inspector Kennedy selected the team he wanted to take to Darrington Manor. A search warrant had been signed by the local magistrate. The police sniffer dogs had been seconded onto the team, and WPC Wendy Jones and PC Baines plus four other officers were all ready to make the visit by one.

Rather than descend mob handed at the Manor, the Inspector instructed his team to wait in the lay-by on the main road, while the Inspector and Sergeant Robbins asked initial questions and presented the search warrant. He wanted to gauge the first reactions of the Miss Carbury's.

Paul Kennedy rang the front door bell. They heard the clip clop of footsteps across the interior hall.

The door was opened by a woman.

'Good afternoon, Miss Carbury, I presume?'

The woman looked a bit puzzled.

'Yes, who are you?' She asked.

'Inspector Kennedy and Sergeant Robbins, Palmouth Police,' he said brandishing his identity badge.

'We would like to ask you and your sister some questions, we also have a warrant to search these premises.'

Fenella visibly paled. 'I am afraid it's not convenient at the moment.'

They heard a female voice shout from the top of the stairs, 'Fenella who is it? Tell them we are busy.'

The Inspector stepped inside the hall and nodded to Clive, who immediately sent the text summoning the troops.

He addressed the large woman, who was rushing down the stairs, 'Miss Carbury, we need to speak to you and your sister and we also have a search warrant for these premises.'

Celeste Carbury, on reaching the bottom of the stairs, tried to physically push the Inspector out of the front door.

'Miss Carbury, if you physically abuse me or any of my officers, I will have no choice other than to arrest you and your sister.'

Fenella started to cry, 'Oh dry up Fenella,' Celeste said harshly to her snivelling sister. She turned round and marched back up the stairs followed by her sister.

The rest of Paul Kennedy's team arrived at the front door. He had primed them on what they were looking for. PC Baines had been delegated to look for a recent bonfire in the grounds and also a well.

The Inspector and WPC Jones followed the two women up the stairs, leaving Sergeant Robbins to co-ordinate the rest of the search.

Celeste once in her office refused to comment at any of the Inspectors questions. Fenella continued to sniff.

WPC Wendy Jones found the room that was obviously the place that Georgina had been incarcerated. She found the upturned bottle of olive oil that the Inspector had told her about. Also, the window was just closed down but the catch was not closed and covered in the oil.

However, she could not see any trace of the doctor's bag that Georgina had described or the over coat.

It was frustrating getting the 'no comment' replies from both sisters and Paul was getting angry at the sneering remarks Celeste was throwing at him.

Sergeant Robbins put his head in the door and asked to speak to Paul. He left WPC Alice Woodrow with the sisters, she had accompanied the Sergeant from downstairs.

Outside the office, Clive told his boss that some buttons had been found and pieces of tweed at the site of a recent bonfire. Also, PC Baines had found the well and was in the process of retrieving what looked like the missing doctor's bag.

Just then, another officer ran up the stairs, 'Guv, the dogs have found something in the area where the new grass has been sewn. Can you authorise a dig? Its Buster, the cadaver dog that has gone crazy.'

Inspector Kennedy nodded, 'Get the boys started and be careful, we need all the evidence bagged as you go.'

He went back into the office, where Celeste was still looking confident.

'Miss Carbury, I think it's time we take a little trip to the station.'

'I am not going anywhere copper.' With that she leapt up and ran into the open cupboard room, slamming the door behind her. Paul heard a bolt go across on the inside of the door.

Clive Robbins had seen what had happened and laughed.

'I can't see that one leaping out of the window, can you guv? Like our other 'old dears'?'

'PC Woodrow will you accompany Miss Fenella downstairs with Sergeant Robbins and take her to Palmouth station, she is to be kept away from her sister.'

Fenella got almost hysterical, and had to be manhandled down the stairs.

'Send two of the boys up here as you go down Clive, with a battering ram, we need to remove the other lady.'

The whole search took over two hours and a van full of bagged items were taken to the station for forensic examination.

The two women were put in separate interview rooms.

A man's body was found buried where the old cess pit had been removed. The bag retrieved from the well proved to belong to Dr Choudery.

Fenella Carbury became a blubbering mess. She said that she didn't know what was going on and blamed everything on Celeste. Celeste herself still refused to make any comment.

Inspector Kennedy asked her about Dr Choudery, but still nothing from Celeste. It wasn't until he mentioned Jason Bishop, did he get any response.

'Was Jason Bishop a boyfriend?' He asked.

Celeste sneered and said, 'I wouldn't touch him with a barge pole.'

'Are you saying that he didn't fancy you? We thought he liked big busted ladies? He tried hard enough to get his girlfriends to have their busts enlarged. I suppose you have had the operation?'

At this, Celeste leapt up from her chair, 'That bastard, he tried to molest me in the park, but I soon sorted him out.'

'I don't believe Jason Bishop would fancy you Celeste, he liked the younger girls,' Paul was trying to goad her.

'That's what you know. He came on to me, tried to put his hand down my front and grab my tits, he pushed me over, my shoe came off, so I whacked him with my shoe. Waste of a Labouton, but I gave him a good thrashing!'

The heel of her spiky shoe explained the injuries Bishop had received.

'So you killed him Miss Carbury?'

'It was self-defence, try and prove different. I want my solicitor; I am saying nothing else.'

Fenella Carbury told a different story. It was a story of years of being bullied by her sister, but she was aware of the cheap implants. Her sister had bought them from a dubious contact she had known in America. Fenella told them that Celeste was a trained surgical nurse and she assisted Dr Choudery in the implant operations. But when he refused to use the second-rate implants, they had a serious argument.

'She told me that Dr Choudery had suffered a heart attack while they were arguing, but I didn't believe her. She has a terrible temper.'

Fenella confirmed that Jason had been summoned to the Manor the same evening, but she didn't know why.

She denied knowing what happened to Choudery or how he died.

'What do you know about the death of Jason Bishop?' the Inspector asked her.

She told them that Celeste had arranged to meet Jason in the park on the night he died. She said she was going to get the money he owed them for Glenys Perry's operation. But Celeste had told her sister that Jason had refused to pay and told Celeste that she owed him for getting rid of Mr Choudery's body.

'Celest told me that he had tried to grab hold of her. She had fallen over and she had hit him with her shoe and was able to escape.'

Both interviews with both women went on for several hours.

Fenella broke down and a doctor had to be called. Her interview was stopped on medical grounds. It appeared she had been on anti-depressants for years and had suffered psychotic episodes.

At ten that night, Celeste Carbury was charged with the murder of Kalib Choudery and Jason Bishop, Fenella was charged with aiding and abetting. It was unlikely that Fenella would ever get to court, as her mental stability was questionable.

'Thank God, that's over,' Paul Kennedy said to Clive Robbins. 'I suppose tomorrow I will have to go and eat humble pie with the two old dears!' He said.

Clive laughed, 'They weren't as batty as I thought, so I had better go with you guv.'

Georgina and Harriet felt completely drained after reliving their adventures for the statement to the police.

Jim had stayed for about half an hour after the police left. He regaled them with a few stories about Inspector Kennedy as a young PC and made them laugh. It was obvious that he had a great affection for the Inspector.

It had been a big surprise to Georgina and Harriet that Jim had once been a policeman. Although he had been born in the cottage where he now lived, during his years on the force he had lived on the other side of Palmouth. He had moved back to the family cottage after his parents had died. He had lived there with his wife until two years ago, when his wife had sadly died. He had never advertised to the village what his occupation had been, although some of the older ones probably knew.

Georgina spent an hour or so in her back garden using some of the advice that Agnes had given her.

Then she had gone indoors when a few spots of rain had curtailed the gardening. Harriet had played with her dogs in the garden then gone inside watched a bit of tv and promptly fell asleep.

Both women had wondered about the police visit to Darrington Manor, but hoped that the information they had unearthed had helped.

An early night was received with great pleasure by Dino, as he snuggled down with Georgina.

Although Harriet had nodded off watching tv, she still had no trouble in sleeping that night.

The next morning, when Georgina called into Martindales stores to pick up her paper, she was delighted to see Janie.

'Hi Janie, nice to see you back.'

Janie smiled and looked a much happier girl. 'Hello Mrs Wright, Nelson is going to get his job back at the packing factory and Teddy is being spoilt rotton by mum.'

'That is brilliant Janie,' Georgina said.

'I am going to see the owner of Maria Collins hairdressers in Palmouth. They have told me I could start as an apprentice hairdresser. I will have to go to college one day a week, but mum says she will look after Teddy for me. We will pay her rent, so she won't have to wash pots in the pub anymore.'

Georgina gave her a hug and told her to bring Janice and Teddy over for tea one day soon.

She couldn't wait to tell Harriet the good news.

As she went out of the shop door, Gloria Partland was about to enter the shop.

'Hello Mrs Wright. Thanks to you for the help you gave me regarding a small problem I had.

With that she went into the shop.

Georgina didn't know what to say! So, she just smiled and said nothing!

She trotted up Harriet's path to her back door, knocked and went inside.

She told Harriet about Janie and the strange thing Gloria had said.

'How did she know what we did? Perhaps she was just saying thanks for the card! But I don't think so.'

Georgina said. 'Well Sherlock we sorted that out !'

'Elementary my dear, Dr Watson!' Harriet said laughing.

They had only just sat down with their cups of coffee when the Inspector and Clive Robbins knocked on Harriet's door.

'Sorry to disturb you ladies, but we saw Mrs Wright come out of the shop and head for your back door.'

Paul Kennedy stood aside to reveal Clive Robbins standing behind him holding two large bunches of flowers.

'These are to say thank you. We have arrested Celeste Carbury and her sister for the murders of Doctor Choudery, whose body we found, and of Jason Bishop.'

The policemen told the women that they had found indisputable proof of the guilt of the sisters. 'We can't go into details, but without your help girls we would have still been struggling, thank you.'

Harriet made them a quick cup of coffee, as they couldn't stay very long.

As they left, Paul Kennedy said laughing, 'Now I don't want you climbing out of anymore windows for a while girls! And no more bodies ladies!'

He gave them a wink and left.

Harriet sighed 'If only we were twenty years younger!'

'Twenty years Sherlock, we would need to be double that to catch a hunk like that.'

'Bingo tonight?' Georgie said.

'Yes, why not?' So that evening they went to Palmouth to the Bingo Hall.

Lady luck was with them. Georgina won the jackpot prize of £450 pounds.

'We will take one of those coach trip holidays to Bournemouth with the money. We deserve a treat.'

Harriet agreed that would lovely.

As they walked out of the Bingo Hall, they saw Margaret Sharples, so they hung back until she was out of sight.

As they got to the door, they could see a crowd gathering.

'What's going on over there?' Harriet said.

'No more adventures please, Sherlock!' Georgina said laughing.

They walked over to see what everyone was looking at and saw Margaret Sharples standing on a metal bench seat with her arm in the large waste bin by the side of the seat.

'What's up Margaret?' Harriet asked as she pushed through the gathered crowd.

'I had me fish n' chips in Bingo and I always take me'teef' out to eat them. I put them on me serviette. I brought the chip box out here with me and the serviette and bunged 'em in this bin, then I remembered me teef' was in the serviette, so I got to get 'em back, now I can't get me bloody arm out!'

Harriet wanted to laugh, but managed to restrain herself. Just then one of the security men who patrol the car park came along.

He climbed up on the seat and grabbed Margaret round the waist and pulled.

Margaret screamed, 'Your squashing me boobs, you moron!'

The red-faced man jumped down and reached for his phone. He didn't want to be accused of assaulting the old woman.

The fire station was fortunately only a short way down the road and a crew were soon at the scene.

One of the firemen tried the same tactic as the security man with a second pulling the bin in the opposite direction. This only made Margaret squeal again.

'Right there is only one answer,' the leading fireman said, 'We will have to cut it off!'

Margaret looked horrified.

'It's ok Margaret, I think he means the bin, not your arm,' Georgina said holding Margaret's other hand.

One of the firemen approached with an evil looking tool and started to carefully remove the top of the bin.

Margaret's arm was soon set free as the top of the bin came away.

She leant forward and stretched down into the bin, gave herself a little heave up with her knees and disappeared into the bin. All they could see was Margaret's legs, adorned with her wrinkly stockings held up by the pink suspenders from her corsets and her long baggy knickers.

One of the firemen tipped the bin onto its side and another pulled Margaret out.

She was beaming and holding aloft her teeth, she was covered in the remains of someone's discarded vindaloo, some chips in her hair and a crisp bag attached to her shoulder.

'Thank you so much lads,' she said, and she pushed her teeth back into her mouth and trotted off to catch the bus that had pulled up at the nearby bus stop.

'Did she really just do that?' Georgina asked aghast.

'Yep, she sure did.'

'Yuk, let's go home and plan our holiday in Bournemouth and sanity.'

'Don't count on it Mrs Marple,' Harriet said, and they drove home.

The Following Week

Harriet went to Martindale's shop to collect the daily papers. As she went into the shop, Jim Talbot followed her.

'Good morning, Harriet,' he said.

'Good morning, Jim, how are you?'.

'I am fine thanks. I was looking at that poster on the board outside the shop. The coach trip to a hotel in Bournemouth.'

'Oh, Jim why don't you book up. Georgina and I are going. It will be a nice break. There are some nice trips on the bus while we are there.'

Jim thought for a minute, 'I will write down the phone number and give them a ring when I get home. I was a little worried that I might not know anyone, but if you and Georgina are going, I will definitely book if there are any places left.'

Harriet got her newspaper and also Georgina's, as she was on her way over to see her friend.

The proposed holiday in Bournemouth was a relaxation week to get over the stress from the murder investigation.

Georgina saw Harriet walking up her garden path and went to her kitchen and put the kettle on.

'Good morning, Mrs Holt,' Georgina said. 'You have got that look on your face, what have you been up to?'

'Not guilty, m'lud. I have just seen Jim and he was contemplating going to Bournemouth on our trip. When I told him we were going, he went back home to see if there are any spare seats.'

Georgina laughed, 'That will be nice to have Jim with us. I think he fancies you, Harry.'

Harriet blushed, but said nothing. She did quite like old Jim.

Jim often called in to one or the other, for a chat and a cup of tea, they often laughed about the cat-napping episode.

Georgina made the coffee and got out the ginger biscuits that they were both partial to. They had just sat down, when Jim popped his head in the kitchen door. They never bothered to knock on each other's doors in the day time when they called on each other.

'Hello girls. I got through to the coach firm and there was a spare seat. They have booked me up with a single room in the hotel, so it's alright ladies, we won't have to share.' Jim laughed and sat down at the kitchen table opposite Harriet, as Georgina poured out his coffee.

'We are so pleased you are coming on the trip Jim. We will have some fun!'

'Now listen Harriet, none of us are climbing out of windows ever again,' Georgina said.

Jim nodded 'I'll be keeping an eye on you both, it's a good job I am coming, I think.'

The holiday was in ten days' time. The next day, they went into Palmouth to buy a few new things. It was only May, but the forecast was good. Neither of them had any thoughts of swimming, even if it became very hot. Georgina hated getting her hair wet although, she could swim but it had never been a favourite occupation. Whereas Harriet couldn't swim although, she would like to have been brave enough to learn, but never seemed to find the time.

The purchases were a comfortable pair of walking shoes each, a warm cardigan and some 'decent' nightwear.

'My pyjamas are tatty,' Harriet said. 'The little dog has chewed holes in my dressing gown, so I had better get a new one, or else the hotel will think we are country bumpkins.'

Georgina bought two new winceyette nighties, which she preferred to pyjamas.

Nine days later, both their cases were packed. Jim like to travel light and just had a large hold-all. They had been told to wait at the bus stop in Gorlstone on Saturday morning at ten. The weather forecast was good for the week, but they had put their umbrellas in, just in case.

The Journey to Bournemouth

At five past ten, a coach arrived. The driver got out and took their cases and stowed them in the luggage space under the bus. Then he assisted them to climb the steps into the bus.

'I think he thinks we are geriatrics,' whispered Georgina, as they sat in a seat about half way along the bus.

Harriet and Jim laughed. Jim had found a seat two seats in front of them. As the bus started, Harriet started to hum 'We're all going on a summer holiday.'

A mile or so up the road the bus pulled into the side of the road at a bus stop.

Jim turned round in his seat and then got up and came back to sit in the seat across the aisle from Georgina and Harriet.

'Do you mind if I sit here next to my friends?' He asked the woman who sat next to the window.

'No, not at all,' she said coyly to Jim.

Jim turned to Harriet and said, 'Look who is getting on the bus!'

Harriet half stood up and saw Margaret Sharples talking to the driver.

Georgina said, 'Quick where's our newspaper?'

She grabbed the paper from her bag and gave Harriet part of it, and they both hid behind the paper. Jim also had turned to speak to the lady who sat beside him, turning his face, hoping that Margaret would not recognise him.

Fortunately, Margaret found a seat near the front of the bus, next to one of a group of youngsters.

'Panic over,' Georgina said laughing putting the newspaper back together.

Harriet got out one of her paperback novels to read, while Georgina sat and looked at their fellow passengers.

At the front of the bus were the group of young people. Four girls and three boys. A man and woman seemed to be in charge of them. The adults had the front seat with the two of the boys sitting opposite, and the four girls on two seats behind the adults, the other boy had sat alone behind his friends across from the girls, until Margaret plonked herself down next to him.

Behind them were a male and female, man and wife Georgina thought. The woman was dressed in a pink suit with a highly ornate matching hat, with a curling feather on top.

'Highly inappropriate,' Georgina thought, 'More fitting for a wedding outfit.' The woman had already made her presence felt. Her voice was like a fog horn and her poor husband obviously had to pay attention to her conversation. Although, he looked as though he would rather be somewhere else.

When the bus arrived at Palmouth, the rest of the seats filled up, but not with people that Georgina or Harriet knew. Jim thought he recognised one or two from his days spent in Palmouth police station as an Inspector, but no-one he could put a name to.

The journey to Bournemouth took about one and a half hour and as the bus approached Bournemouth, the sun shone. The coach drove up to the East Cliff, everyone was looking at the wonderful views. The sea was a lovely azure blue, the sky very clear.

'Look Harriet, you can see the Isle of Wight.'

The bus pulled into the driveway of the hotel and the passengers started to get ready to vacate the bus.

The First Day

It boded well for their little holiday break. The hotel 'The Blue Chine' looked out over a scenic view towards the Purbeck hills to the west, and you could just see the Isle of Wight on the horizon. To the left, was Hengistbury Head, their coach driver told them, a very ancient settlement where Iron Ore had been excavated.

The hotel was a large white-washed building with a crenelated roof. Obviously, a relic from earlier times, but looked well maintained.

They all got off the coach and collected their cases and went into the hotel.

The interior of the hotel was not disappointing. Nice bright décor and well-presented reception staff greeted them.

Georgina and Harriet were given the key to their room and shown the lift to their room, which was on the second floor. Jim was also on the same floor and just two rooms away from them, down the corridor.

They were all pleased to have rooms with a sea view and en-suite facilities, even Jim in his single room had his own shower room.

They were told that after they had freshened up, there was a welcome meeting with refreshments waiting for them in the dining room.

As the three friends descended in the lift, Margaret Sharples entered the lift on the first floor along with an elderly gent who had been on their bus. She hardly noticed Harriet and Georgina and was intent on talking to the old man in a loud voice.

'I won't put up with it, I will tell them so too. Giving me one of those duvvit things, I like my candlewick and a proper sheet on my bed!'

The old gent seemed not to respond.

'Do you hear what I said to you?' Margaret shouted.

The old boy looked up at Margaret, 'Speak up woman. What do you want a candle for?'

Harriet wanted to laugh and was grateful that the lift had reached the ground floor. Georgina took her arm and escaped the lift and made for the dining room.

'Margaret's pulled then!' Harriet said laughing.

The old gent that Margaret had taken charge of, had got on their bus in Palmouth and had sat behind Margaret on the bus, on his own.

The travel representative was in the dining room about to give the guests a short talk on what the holiday offered, while they were offered sandwiches and cakes as a welcome to Bournemouth.

It appeared there were two trips were offered free with the holiday. One to Salisbury and Stonehenge. They would have a drive-by of the stones, and then be dropped off in Salisbury near the cathedral and given two hours to explore the cathedral and the city.

The other trip was to Portland and Weymouth. They could have coffee in the café at Portland Bill and then be taken down to Weymouth, where they could have lunch and an ice cream before returning to Bournemouth.

The hotel offered a free mini bus ride down to the town and beach in Bournemouth, leaving at ten every morning or two in the afternoon.

'Well, that should be a nice trip. I have never been to Salisbury. Have seen the Constable painting and the cathedral looks amazing. I suppose it's good to say you have seen Stonehenge, but more interested in seeing the cathedral,' Georgina said.

'Once you've seen one pile of stones, you've seen them all,' Jim said.

'Shall we have a stroll along the front and look at the views?' Harriet suggested after the travel rep had finished her talk and they had had a snack. They all agreed that it would be a good idea.

They could hear Margaret shouting at her companion, as they left the hotel, but it didn't seem as though he heard a lot of what she said.

After their walk, Harriet, Georgina and Jim sat with their cups of tea in the conservatory that ran along the front of the hotel. It was nice just to relax.

They decided that they would have a quiet day and plan the next day. The hotel offered entertainment after the evening meal, so a snooze and a read of the paper was enjoyed by all three of them on that first afternoon.

The chairs in the hotel conservatory were very comfortable and upholstered in a pretty pink draylon. It wasn't long before all three of them were snoozing.

Harriet had dropped off for a sleep first, but was the first to open her eyes.

As she opened her eyes, she looked across the road and saw a man and a woman with a purple scarf round her shoulders on the far side of the road, who seemed to be having words. She thought she recognised both of them, as two of her fellow guests who had been on their coach. But as she hadn't got her glasses on, she wasn't sure.

The woman waved her fist at the man and pushed him in the chest and hurried off towards Bournemouth. The man staggered back at the ferocity of the shove he received on his chest, he then turned and walked in the opposite direction.

'Strange!' Harriet thought. Then she picked her book up and decided to leave Jim and Georgina to their nap, and went up to the room to have a long soak in the bath before it was time for dinner.

As she waited for the lift, the group of four girls and the woman who had been on the bus with Georgina and Harriet came to wait for the lift. The girls were all excitedly chattering.

'They are excited as we are going over to Brownsea Island tomorrow. We have hired two tents and they are going to have their first night under canvas. I am Beatrice Jones, their Brown Owl leader, from Darrington he told Harriet.

'Rather you than me. I would be afraid of creepy crawlies,' Harriet shuddered at the thought.

'My colleague Mr Bunt, the scout leader has three boys who are also coming over to the island. We will get him to remove any uninvited guests in our tent. Nice to meet you,' she said, extending her hand for a handshake and then giggled. 'Boris is very good with the bugs!' Then giggled again.

'Blimey,' thought Harriet, she fancies Mr Bunt. Harriet smiled to herself at the thought of Beatrice and Boris shacked up in a tent. Her imagination running wild!

The lift descended and the chattering girls, Harriet and Miss Jones piled into the lift. The girls and their leader left the lift on the first floor.

By the time Harriet had finished her bath, Georgina had arrived and was preparing for her shower. She preferred a shower, whereas Harriet liked to wallow, as she put it, in the bath.

'I should have shaved my legs before we came on holiday,' Harriet said.

'Why bother? Who is going to look at our legs?' Georgina said, as she went into the bathroom.

'I live in hope,' Harriet said, as she rummaged in her toilet bag for the safety razor she hoped to find there.

Although, both the women happily lived alone, each in their own home, both often talked of, that maybe one day they would each find another partner.

Harriet had been widowed several months before Georgina. They had supported each other through the loss of each of their husbands.

Harriet was sitting on her bed thinking about their lives. She had a certain look on her face, Georgina asked her what she was thinking about. Harriet had a history of 'dopey ideas' and Georgie was apprehensive about what was going through her pal's mind!

'I don't think there are any George Clooney look-alikes on our bus, they all seem to be taken or miserable looking buzzards,' she said.

'Jim is keen on you Harry, you know that.'

Harriet smiled, 'I was thinking of you, someone to make up a foursome.'

'I could always seduce Margaret's beau, the old deaf bat!'

They both laughed, 'Think Margaret would fight you for him. 'Walking sticks at dawn!' Remember the last time we looked for a man? That didn't end well.'

Romeo, Wherefore Art Thou?

Georgina sat on her bed and they reminisced.

They had joined a dating site for seniors. It had been a laugh to start with.

They had come to the conclusion that being a widow made them two of an ever-increasing band of desperate women. Which neither really was, but being on the dating site had been more entertainment than desperation.

They had a plan. On receiving a contact from an interested party, they would take it in turns to reply. They had concocted a profile that could apply to either of them. Submitted a photo that was at some distance, height and weight somewhere between the two of them. Harriet being taller and chunkier, so medium build and halfway height between their two actual statistics had been the input. They had laughed so much filling out the profile, that in itself had proved amusing.

The first applicant to contact them had caused hilarious laughter. A twenty something male from Africa. The thought of a toy boy hadn't crossed their minds, and was quickly dispatched by the delete button.

The second applicant had sounded a possibility. Tall, around the same age as the girls. A retired railwayman. His picture had seemed a little suspect, but perhaps he had led a charmed life and kept the wrinkles at bay.

Harriet had drawn the short straw, as to who was going to actually meet this man, who went by the name of Neville. The arranged meeting place was to be at the front door of a garden centre, prior to a cup of tea in the café.

Georgina was to go and sit in the café, while Harriet waited outside for Neville.

Georgina bought a cup of tea and started to read her newspaper keeping a watchful eye on the 'proceedings'. They had arranged that Harriet would drop her serviette on the floor if she needed rescuing.

Georgina had disappeared into the café ten minutes before the appointed time, and Harriet sat in her car shivering with fear.

She had seen a tall man approach the doorway; he looked a little like Sean Connery. Harriet felt hopeful, but this chap had waited holding the door open for a gorgeous looking female with a skirt so short, you could practically see her knickers!

Harriet had got out of her car and approached the doorway. Suddenly from nowhere came a booming voice.

'Alice is that you?' Alice was the alias her and Georgina had decided on.

Harriet turned round to see a tall old man marching towards her. His face was like a crumpled tissue. The photo on the site must have been many years ago.

Harriet had smiled and held out her hand to shake his, but he had grabbed her arm and marched her into the garden centre.

'Come along my dear, it's time for food.'

Harriet had trotted alongside and said, 'A nice cup of tea will be nice.'

'Tea? Its lunch time woman!'

He got a tray and thrust another into Harriet's hands.

He had ordered a double jacket potato with chilli con carne. Harriet decided although not particularly hungry, to have a jacket potato with cheese on top.

Along with a large coffee for himself and a cup of tea for her, they proceeded to the pay desk.

The assistant totalled up the amount due and suddenly Neville patted his pockets, 'Oh dash it, have left my wallet in my car and its right at the back of the car park. You sort this out old girl, I will see you right when we go out.'

Harriet hadn't wanted to look a complete idiot, so she handed the assistant her credit card.

'Well done old thing!' Neville boomed.

They had taken a table not far from where Georgina was sitting.

She was trying not to laugh. Harriet wanted so badly to hit her!

Neville gave her an in-depth history of his achievements, it appeared that British Rail as it was then, would have ground to a complete halt without Neville.

He then continued seeming not to draw breath to give her the entire instructions of how to reverse a steam engine and the difference between driving a diesel engine and a steam train.

Harriet had tried desperately not to yawn.

Harriet ate her potato, but although Neville had twice as much on his plate he had still finished long before she did, even though he hadn't stopped lecturing her.

Harriet never ate the skin of a jacket potato, much to Neville's disgust.

'You not eating that skin woman?' Harriet had shaken her head and before she could speak, her plate was snatched away and the offending skin was devoured by her escort. For a moment she thought he was going to lick her plate clean. Instead, he ran his finger round the plate to pick up the remains of a few cheese crumbs that Harriet had dared to leave!

Harriet was speechless. She had looked across at Georgina, who was almost doubled up trying not to laugh.

'I hate you Georgie, I really hate you,' Harriet had thought.

Then she then remembered the napkin dropping arrangement. But too late, Neville was blowing his nose on it!

'Excuse me Neville, I would like to go to the powder room.' Harriet had got up and as she'd walked towards the toilets, she heard Neville speak, as did all the other diners, 'Alright old girl, the water works dodgy, it happens you know at our age!'

Harriet had kept walking clutching her handbag. The desire to hit him over the head receding as she'd got nearer the toilets.

Georgina left her table and followed Harriet.

When Georgina got into the toilets, she was met with Harriet's backside disappearing through the toilet window. She went to the window and looked out only to see Harriet's legs sticking out of a large hydrangea.

Georgina had not been keen on exiting the toilets the same way as Harriet, so she went out of the toilets and left the garden centre as soon as she could. She had found a very dishevelled Harriet unlocking her car and was instructed to get in quickly. They made a very hasty retreat from the centre. Harriet very soon recovered her sense of humour, but her thoughts on Neville and the dating game were unrepeatable and definitely not lady-like!

The two women sitting in their beds in the hotel bedroom giggled like two school girls.

'Windows seem to attract you, old bean! I wonder what happened to Neville?' Georgina said.

'I don't know and I don't care,' Harriet said, 'What about your garden gnome?'

'Oh don't Harriet, I had nightmares after that.'

The next applicant for their affections had been Harold. He sounded quite pleasant and the smiling photo was of an older man with receding hair.

Georgina had said that he didn't look like a mass murderer.

Harriet had asked what one of those looked like.

They decided to be brave and agreed to meet Harold, this was Georgina's turn. Harriet wickedly secretly hoped that it would be her turn to laugh.

They had chosen a different garden centre, just in case Neville was prowling around. Same arrangement as before, with Harriet going into café first and Georgie meeting Harold at the front door.

Georgina had sat in her car, which at the time was a 4x4. She picked up the phone intending to phone Harriet to make sure she had found a table in the café. She had her phone in her hand when she heard a voice.

'Hello are you phoning me?'

Georgina looked around she couldn't see anyone.

She started to dial then, 'Hello, are you Alice?'

Georgina still couldn't see anyone, so she opened her car door. There was a groan, and she realised that her car door had knocked someone into the hedge.

As she stepped down from her vehicle, she saw a pair of legs sticking out of the privet hedge that surrounded the car park.

A very small man extracted himself from the hedge straightened himself up and bounded up to Georgina.

'Hi, I am Harold.'

Georgina viewed her prospective beau. He had a hand knitted woolly jumper in canary yellow decorated with a knitted robin and a matching bobble hat without the robin.

Georgina swallowed, knowing full well that Harriet would enjoy her discomfort. Harold could only be about four feet and ten inches tall.

'I am sorry I knocked you over Harold, but I didn't know you were so close to my car door,' she had said, as he stood beside her looking up at her, still picking pieces of the hedge out of his jumper.

'Oh no worries, mother always says I get in her way at times. Shall we go to the café for a cup of tea?'

Georgina led the way, walking in front of little Harold hoping that people wouldn't know they were actually together.

'At least if we sit down, he won't look so small' she thought. Then she caught sight of a child's high chair as they went into the café, but dismissed the thought that went through her mind!

Harriet caught sight of them at the counter as Harold paid for their tea. A big grin had gone across her face, which she quickly hid behind the menu she was reading.

Georgina wondered how big the windows were in the ladies, then remembered the serviette routine they had talked about. At least Harold wasn't wiping his nose on it!

She had sipped her tea while Harold started to tell her about his mother's varicose veins, and alopecia. She'd picked up the serviette and let it slip through her fingers onto the floor.

Harriet was enjoying her friend's situation so much that she thought, 'This is revenge for the Neville incident!'

So, she let a few minutes pass before she got her mobile out of her bag and dialled Georgie's number.

Georgina grabbed her phone and although Harriet had not spoken, Georgina said, 'Hello. Oh, dear you poor thing. Yes of course I can come and fetch you. I am at the Garland Garden Centre but I can be there within twenty minutes. Don't worry.'

She replaced the phone in her bag, finished her tea and looked sadly at Harold.

'I am so sorry that was my daughter. She has twisted her ankle and needs to get to A and E. I will have to go and pick her up.'

Before Harold could speak, Georgina had stood up, shaken Harold's hand and told him it had been lovely to meet him and rushed out of the garden centre, followed by a grinning Harriet.

Harriet and Georgina had given up the dating ideas after that, but even now they could still laugh about the situations.

Evening Dinner

Georgina went to have her shower while Harriet rummaged through her suitcase to decide on her ensemble for the evening.

'I suppose we had better get dressed and go down and join the merry band for our evening meal.'

Georgina always looked smart, and co-ordinated her outfits to perfection. Harriet on the other hand went for comfort, the colour mixes were of little worry to her. Whatever came out of her case she was happy with, as long as she was warm.

Georgina put on a Marks and Spencer navy skirt with matching jacket with a pretty white blouse and navy court shoes.

Harriet put on a floral skirt with pink flowers and a long green t-shirt. She put on a pair of open-toed sandals to complete her outfit.

'That will do. Covers my fat up a bit!' She said.

Georgina was quite used to Harriet's dress code and it didn't bother her at all.

The two ladies locked their room door and went along the corridor to the lift. As they went past room no. 37, they could hear someone shouting.

'Just get out of here and keep your mouth shut, or else,' A male voice said.

'You know what to do or your wife will get a lovely surprise,' A female voice replied. The two women realised that someone was about to open the door where the altercation was taking place. They trotted away from the door to the opening lift. Harriet looked back out of the lift and saw one of the hotel staff rush out of the room and go back along the corridor.

'Oh, what was that all about then?' Georgina said. 'Did you see who came out of that room?'

Harriet nodded, 'It was one of the maids, I think. Don't know who is staying in that room, do you?'

Georgina didn't know, and they carried on down to the dining room for their dinner.

The food was very good with a varied selection. The tables were tastefully dressed each with a small spill vase containing a real flower.

'Makes a change to see a real flower, generally you get a plastic one.' Georgina sniffed the flower and replaced it back in the middle of the table.

The tables were placed fairly close to each other and they were relieved to see that Margaret Sharples was sitting at the other side of the room along with the deaf old gent that she had seemed to have monopolised. On the table to their right were a couple that had got on the bus in Palmouth.

Harriet nodded to them as they sat down. The man seemed in the same age group as both Harriet and Georgina. He stood up and came over to their table.

'Good evening, ladies. Major Herbert Rammidges and my lady wife Felicity.'

He took Harriet's hand, shaking it strongly, then went round to Georgina, who proffered her hand gingerly.

'Harriet Holt and Georgina Wright.'

The major took her hand raised it to his lips and said, 'Charmed, I am sure ladies.'

Georgina waited till the Major had resumed his seat then she wiped her hand on her serviette, shuddering.

Harriet grinned, 'Oops, look like you have an admirer.'

Mrs Rammidges, the lady wife nodded her head then quickly looked away.

'It couldn't have been the Major we heard yelling at the chamber maid as they were already sat at their table when we got here,' Georgina said.

At the table, on the other side of the women, sat the woman who had been on their bus dressed ready for a wedding. Tonight, she was wearing an ornate turban with swathes of pearls adorning a flowery dress and jacket. Her husband came into the restaurant and took his seat next to the woman. Harriet smiled at the woman, 'Good evening.'

The woman prodded her husband, 'Go and introduce us to these nice ladies, they at least look like respectable people, unlike some of them in this establishment.'

The husband came across to Harriet and Georgina's table and held out his hand. 'Dennis and Gert, I mean Trudi Rabitay.'

Georgina shook his hand and made the introduction. Harriet nodded and smiled.

Harriet looked mischievous. 'We got a slimy major on one side and a rabbit family on the other!' She said quietly.

Georgina laughed and suddenly noticed Jim coming across the room to their table. 'Hi girls. Sorry, I went up to my room and sat on my bed and dropped off to sleep. Have you met any of our fellow holidaymakers yet?'

Georgina glared at Harriet as she guessed what she was about to say.

Most of the other passengers from the bus had now taken their seats in the restaurant.

Miss Madget, the single lady, who Jim had sat next to on the bus was sharing a table with a couple of the small girls, and seemed to be enjoying talking with them. Jim had told them that Lydia Madget was a primary school teacher and was hoping to meet up with an aged aunt who lived near Bournemouth.

'A seemingly shy young woman,' Jim told them.

The other youngsters were sat at a larger table along with the two adults who seemed to be in charge of them.

The two very elderly ladies that had got on the bus in Palmouth were sitting at a table near to Margaret and the old gent, that she seemed to have commandeered.

Another couple who had been on the bus when Harriet, Georgina and Jim had got on the bus, came into the restaurant and took a table near to the stage.

Also, a youngish chap followed them in and sat with the couple.

'I know that young man on his own,' Jim said. 'His parents run the kennels where young Letticia works, I think he is an accountant, He lives in Darrington'.

'I wonder why a young man would come on a coach trip on his own?' Georgina said.

'Perhaps he was hoping there would be some youngsters on board, instead of us geriatrics,' Harriet said laughing.

As they ate their dinner, Georgina told Jim about the row they had heard earlier. He hadn't heard any of it, as his room was further away than theirs.

'Oh well we have left our detective hats in Gorlstone so we are going to have a restful holiday!' Harriet said, ' Now what's the plan for tomorrow gang?'

They discussed the plan for the following day, while enjoying the very good menu. The plan was to go on the trip to Weymouth the following day. The rep had explained that they would be taken onto the Isle of Portland for a sight-seeing tour, ending at the café at Portland Bill, where they could get refreshments.

'We are leaving at ten in the morning, so perhaps a coffee at the café, then when we get to Weymouth, we could have fish and chips,' Jim said. He liked his food and living on his own it was a pleasure to have his food prepared for him.

'Sounds good to me,' said Georgina.

After they had finished their dinner, they went to the room next door to the dining room. There was a bar and a four-piece band had assembled to entertain them with music and there was a space should any of the guests like to have a dance. Possibly because it was the first evening, no-one ventured onto the floor. Also, the food had been so plentiful, the guest all seemed happy to enjoy the music. One of the band members, did a short amusing spot where he told a few jokes. He then encouraged the guests to sing along with a few old favourites. Both Harriet, Georgina and Jim sang along and soon began to feel drowsy.

'I think I will soon go up. All this food and the sea air is making me sleepy,' said Jim. The girls were feeling the same, so they went up to their rooms at about nine.

As they got out of the lift, they saw a couple going into number 37 in front of them. It was the Rabitays.

'That's the room where we heard the shouting earlier. But they looked like quite staid couple,' Harriet told Jim.

'I thought I recognised the man when I got on the bus, but I can't bring it to mind why I thought I know him,' Jim said.

Jim, a retired police Inspector and had a good memory for faces.

The door to number 37 was shut by the time they passed by. They said goodnight to Jim as they arrived at their door, his was two doors further along the corridor.

The ladies got ready for bed. The room had two three quarter beds in and looked exceedingly comfortable. After a few minutes tucked up in their beds, they soon put their lights off and were soon asleep.

Day Two

The weather on the second day looked very promising. Harriet went to the window of their room and the view was breath taking. The Purbeck Hills were to the right, looking misty through the early morning haze. Georgina jumped out of bed and joined her at the window. 'Looks like it's going to be another lovely day. You can see the Isle of Wight from here, see the Needles sticking out into the sea. A nice day to go to Weymouth.'

'What's that place there on the left, all that green hillside. It looks quite high.'

The driver said it was called Hengistbury Head. It was a Stone Age settlement apparently.'

'Harriet laughed and said, 'Perhaps we will have a walk over there before we go home.'

They both got washed and dressed and put their camera's in their handbags.

'Should we take a brolly with us just in case?' Georgina asked.

'I have put my fold up one in my bag, but I think it will be fine.' Harriet said.

They walked along the corridor towards the lift. As they got to number 37, the door opened and Mrs Rabitay walked out. She turned to her husband who followed her from the room. She totally ignored Georgina and Harriet.

Once again, Mrs Rabitay was dressed to kill! This time a pale purple trouser suit with a silk scarf draped around her shoulders. She had a purple turban type creation perched upon her head.

'Come along Dennis, I suppose we have to go on that awful bus again with those plebeians.' Then she stomped off along the corridor to the lift, with her husband trotting on behind.

Harriet looked at Georgina aghast, 'Did she means us? Cheeky bitch!'

Georgina laughed, 'No she said plebeians not lesbians!'

'Oh, that's alright then. What's a plebeian then?'

Georgina tried to explain, but wasn't sure Harriet understood or was even listening.

They had breakfast with Jim who was already sitting at their table. After they had eaten, they went to the rear of the hotel, where their bus was parked. They sat together with Jim across the aisle from them. Miss Madget who had sat next to Jim on the journey to the hotel arrived, and Jim got up and let her sit by the window. She said nothing apart from saying thanks when Jim had stood up to let her get into her seat. She appeared to have brought her knitting bag.

It seemed that most of the original passengers had decided to go on this trip, apart from Mr Bunt and Miss Jones and their charges. Harriet imagined them curled up in their tent together on Brownsea Island.

The over-dressed Rabitay woman and her husband commandeered the front seats.

Harriet was giggling at today's outfit.

'Exactly what one should wear to the seaside!' Harriet remarked.

Jim laughed, 'Hope a seagull doesn't land on it or worse!'

Harriet realised that Mrs Rabitay was the person she had seen having the altercation with the man on the sea front the day before. It was seeing the purple scarf draped round her neck, the same as the woman she had seen.

The man she had been talking to was also getting on the coach. As he walked up the aisle of the coach, passing Jim, Harriet and Georgina, Gert Rabitay turned her face away and looked out of the window. He took a seat towards the rear of the bus.

When the driver checked his list and was sure he had all the passengers that had booked to go on the tour, they drove out of the hotel car park.

Jim tried to include Miss Madget in the conversation, but it became clear she was not a chatty lady. She had her canvas bag on her lap from which she took out her knitting. Jim gave up and watched the scenery as they went along.

It took about an hour to get to get to Portland Bill. They all alighted from the bus, some walked to the little cafe but others walked to the cliff edge. On the way Jim took some photographs of the lighthouse.

Portland Bill is the southern-most tip of the isle of Portland. Very popular with bird watchers. There are three lighthouses two of which have been decommissioned over the years. The shoreline is very rocky with cliffs that periodically erode and fall into the sea.

The tides around the island are treacherous. Shipping is restricted to small fishing craft and leisure boats. A two-mile sandbank makes it impossible for the larger vessels to pass near to the shore.

Although Portland is still referred to as the Isle of Portland, there is a causeway that allows traffic to drive over, so technically not an island.

Shall we go inside the lighthouse and have a look before we go for our coffee?' Georgina said.

'As long as you don't expect me to climb up to the top,' Jim said laughing.

Several of the hotel guests had wandered into the lighthouse, so the three of them followed.

'Some of the guests have gone straight to the café,' said the bus driver Egbert, who had joined Jim and the ladies. They browsed the interesting display of rocks and fossils in the lighthouse and then wandered over towards the cliff edge.

The Rabitays and Miss Madget had also walked over to obelisk, which sat on the cliff edge. Dennis was taking photos of his wife who was clutching her turban and posing. Miss Madget was a few yards away carrying her knitting bag and camera.

Suddenly there was a bang, Gert Rabitay clutched her husband and screamed, 'Someone has just shot at me!' She screamed.

Dennis couldn't see any signs of an injury, and ushered his wife away from the cliff and tried to calm her down.

'Don't be silly Gert,' he said as his wife stormed off towards the café.

Dennis followed receiving a storm of abuse from his furious wife.

'Oops, the rabbit is not happy!'

'Don't get into the habit of calling her that, you could make a mistake when she can hear you,' Georgina said.

They followed Jim and the coach driver and strolled round the white walls that enclosed the lighthouse. Ahead of them they could see several of their fellow tourists wandering towards the cafe.

The Major and his wife were still near the edge of the cliff.

Suddenly the Major shouted, 'Hey look there are some dolphins!'

Jim took a few shots, but it started to rain so the four of them made for the cafe entrance.

The Rabitays had quietened down by the time they all got into the café, although Gert still had a face like thunder.

The major, his wife and Miss Madget soon returned to the café out of the rain. The Major was telling everyone about the dolphins.

Someone shouted, 'Look we can see them from here.'

Everyone except Margaret, her elderly friend and the two old ladies rushed to the café windows with their cameras ready to get a photo.

For several minutes cameras clicked and shrieks of delight could be heard.

The waitress was suddenly she shouted 'Oh my God, somebody do something.'

They turned round from the window and Gert Rabitay was laying across her table.

'Don't touch anything,' Jim said. The policeman in him took control of the situation. He checked her pulse and shook his head.

'Someone call an ambulance,' Jim instructed the café manager who had appeared, 'And I suggest the police as well'.

Jim had spoken to the waitress who had witnessed Mrs Rabitay`s collapse. She had told him that the woman had been sipping her drink when she suddenly grabbed her throat and fallen onto the table.

Jim had been immediately suspicious that this was no medical collapse, hence he had requested they call the police.

Jim took charge of things and ushered everyone in the café to the other side of the room. He put chairs round the area, where Mrs Rabitay's body lay and told everyone not to touch anything.

Harriet and Georgina comforted Lydia Madget, who sat crying. Gavin Thomas the single young man from their group introduced himself to the ladies and asked the waitress to bring more drinks to all the customers.

The Major and his wife shared a table with Margaret Sharples and old Claud. She who was telling everyone that there was a murderer on the loose! Her companion, the old gent was reading a copy of the cafes Times newspaper quite unconcerned, and ignoring Margaret.

The two elderly ladies, who introduced themselves as sisters, Emily and Maud Collins, had not ventured out to the cliff top. They sipped the tea that was brought to them and even asked for a toasted tea cake. The severity of the incident seemed to have gone over their heads.

Margaret Sharples, and the old gent she had attached herself to, Claud Rumsey-Jones also seemed unconcerned about events and Margaret was demanding more tea.

Egbert had given Jim and his two friends the information about their fellow travellers. 'Call me Bert, you can drop the Egg bit, he had said. My father was from Germany and wanted me named after his father. But Bert is fine!'

The other couple who had walked over to the cliffs were Thomas and Erma Williams, a couple from Darrington, originally from Wales. Both seemed very upset over the events.

Dennis Rabitay sat clutching his camera as white as a sheet.

He was a bit of an amateur photographer, and his camera was his most precious possession.

They all sat quietly. Some were chatting, but mostly just sitting sipping their drinks.

A police car arrived and they could see an ambulance driving slowly over to the cafe.

Two policemen entered the café and walked over to the table, where Gert's body lay. The paramedics arrived and examined the body. They spoke quietly to the Inspector, confirming that she was dead and beyond their help. 'Call the forensic team Sergeant, and then we will take details from everyone present. We need to clear the café to allow forensics to do their job.

The Inspector then walked over to where all the group were seated.

He caught sight of Jim, who went to meet Inspector Kennedy.

'Morning Paul. Have moved everyone away and nothing has been touched. Most of us are on a coach trip from Bournemouth.

Jim told the Inspector of his conversation with the waitress who had witnessed Mrs Rabitay`s collapse, 'I think she has been poisoned.'

The Inspector nodded and walked over to the group.

'Ladies and gentlemen, it will be necessary to speak to each of you. My Sergeant will come and take your details and a statement from each of you. We will try and not keep you too long.'

'Blimey Georgie, do you see who the policeman is? What's he doing here?'

Harriet and Georgina turned to look at the police officer.

'Yes, it's Paul Kennedy and Sergeant Robbins from Palmouth,' Jim said.

'They must have been seconded to Bournemouth. The Conservative Party are having a conference in Bournemouth. They usually bring in extra police from surrounding areas'

Georgina said nothing. She was trying to get the picture out of her head.

The paramedic spoke to Paul Kennedy again, before leaving.

'Looks like she was poisoned, but until we get her to the hospital, we can't be sure.'

The café manager opened the doors to the conservatory that was on the side of the café and Sergeant Robbins took members of the group one by one inside to take their statements.

They all had much the same story, they had all rushed to the window to watch the dolphins, Gert Rabitay had gone to look, but went back to her table as animals bored her. On sitting down, she had drunk some of her coffee and then she had collapsed over her table.

Jim shook hands with the Sergeant when his turn came. 'Hello Clive, surprised to see you and Paul Kennedy here. Suppose it's the conference in Bournemouth?'

'Yes, but didn't expect to be called to a possible murder enquiry, but all the local boys are shepherding the politicians around!'

'So, you think she was murdered, thought I smelt the tell-tale smell of almonds. Cyanide I suspect, but good luck, this is your baby.'

'We will come to the hotel for more in depth interviews Jim, but is there anything relevant that you can tell us?'

Jim thought for a minute, 'Well she thought someone took a shot at her when we were out at the cliffside. There was a bang, but I wasn't convinced that it was a gunshot, but she had a screaming fit and her old man brought her over here to the café. She wasn't an easy woman.'

'Interesting Jim, I will have a look in their bags as I interview them, in case one of the old dears has something they shouldn't about their person!'

As Clive Robbins looked at the group waiting to be interviewed, he caught sight of Harriet and Georgina.

'Oh, not them again! They are magnets to murder, where they turn up there's a body.'

Jim laughed, 'We are on a holiday break to get over the goings on in Gorleston!'

'Better send them in Jim'

Harriet blushed and Georgina tried to smile as they went into the conservatory to give their statement.

They couldn't tell the Sergeant much more than any of the others. He did ask about the supposed gun shot that Gert had panicked over on the cliff top, but neither Harriet or Georgina could tell him much, they had heard the bang but had no idea where it came from. They had gone to the window, as had all the others in the café to view the dolphins and they both thought that everyone had done the same.

After all the statements and details had been taken, Inspector Kennedy told the coach party to return to their bus, but to expect a visit from them at the hotel to take further statements. There were six other customers who had driven to the lighthouse in their own transport. One elderly couple, plus a younger couple and their twin sons who had been taken to the lighthouse, as a birthday treat. Their mother had taken the boys back to their car with the Inspectors permission as a murder scene was not the right place for impressionable little boys.

When the group were all seated back on the bus, minus Dennis Rabitay, who was going to be taken back to their hotel by the police. He was very shaken and was in no fit state to continue on the bus.

Bert, their driver asked them all if they wanted to go into Weymouth as planned, or would they prefer to go straight back to the hotel.

Margaret Sharples immediately said she wanted to go into Weymouth and the others decided that perhaps it would take their minds off the situation. None of them had eaten at the café and Jim mentioned fish and chips, so it was agreed that they would spend a couple of hours as planned in Weymouth.

Everyone was very subdued, but it was a lovely day, Bert dropped them off on the promenade and they found a fish and chip called, The Fish Plaice, nearly opposite the drop off place where they could sit outside. Everyone except Margaret, found a table and ordered their meal. Margaret tried to persuade Claud to go with her to the shops, but he had found himself a chair and was reading the menu.

He waved her away and muttered something at Margaret, all Harriet heard was the last word 'off' as he turned his back on Margaret who very disgruntled, marched off towards the shops.

'Oops,' Harriet said 'Looks like the end of a romance'

Jim and Georgina laughed.

Although a lot of thoughts were in all their minds, it didn't seem to be the place to discuss events. So, they ate their fish and chips and sat and enjoyed the view of the sandy beaches.

After their lunch Georgina, Harriet and Jim had a stroll along the promenade. Then found a seat near to the coach pickup point.

Bert returned to pick his passengers and they all seemed subdued and eager to get back to Bournemouth. Even Margaret Sharples seemed to have taken a vow of silence.

Gathering of Tears and
Trembling of Distress

Lord Byron

When the group got back to the hotel, they all went to their rooms. Harriet and Georgina took their coats off and sat on their beds.

'Well, what do you make of that then Sherlock?' Georgina said.

Harriet was deep in thought, 'It's obvious that she was poisoned. Did you see the way the Sergeant put her coffee cup in a bag, and he was sniffing around her head!'

'Isn't it arsenic or cyanide that leaves a funny smell? No, think it's cyanide, my last Agatha Christie had a poisoning in it and that was cyanide and smelt of almonds. But then it had to be someone in the café that did it, while we were all watching the dolphins.'

'If you think about it, Mrs Rabbit went to the window before us, but then seemed to get bored and returned to her table.' Harriet scratched her head.

'So, anyone else could have passed her table and popped something into her coffee!'

Georgina laughed, 'Have you got your detective hat on again Harry? Don't say anything to Jim'.

They both decided to stay in their room and have a read, which soon turned into a snooze.

That evening at dinner, Dennis Rabitay came into the dining room still looking very grey. Jim had met him as they came down in the lift and asked Dennis if he would like to sit with the two women and himself. He seemed very grateful for the offer.

Neither Harriet or Georgina thought is wise to discuss the events of the day.

Jim asked Dennis about his photography hobby and they discussed types of cameras and lens. When the pudding was served, a tear ran down Dennis's face.

'Apple crumble was Gert's favourite pudding,' he said, trying to pull himself together.

Georgina leant across and put her hand on Dennis's arm.

'We are so sorry Dennis, if you need to talk, we are all good listeners. Jim is a retired police officer so you can be assured that anything you say, will be in confidence.'

Dennis wiped his eyes and said, 'Thank you. Gert wasn't an easy woman to live with and to be truthful, I had wondered if my life would be more peaceful if I went and lived with my brother. He is on his own and we used to go fishing together, although Gert didn't like me going to see him.'

Jim frowned and said, 'Possibly not a good thing to tell the Inspector Dennis. He may think you had reasons to be rid of her!'

After they had eaten their dinner, Dennis excused himself and returned to his room. He said that the doctor had given him something to help him sleep.

Neither Jim, Harriet or Georgina felt like listening to the music in the adjacent room, so they decided to have a short walk along the promenade and watch the sun go down over the Purbecks.

They found an empty wooden bench and just sat.

'Do you think that someone did try and take a pot-shot at Gert at Portland?' Georgina asked Jim.

Jim hesitated before he replied, 'I thought about that, it didn't sound right to me, but we can't rule it out. There were only people from our bus at the cliff top, at the time she screamed, and that woman with the twins. I told Paul Kennedy and he said he was going to search our rooms, here, just in case one of us has a something they shouldn't, he had one of his boys search our bus before we got back on.'

'Sergeant Robbins did look into our handbags when we made our statements at the café, I wondered what he was looking for?' Harriet said.

As they sat on the bench, which was about 50 yards from the hotel, Harriet noticed Gavin Thomas hurrying across the road from the hotel entrance. He had a black carrier bag under his arm. He climbed over the wall that led to the grassy bank that was above the sandy beach below. It all happened so fast Harriet didn't have time to alert Jim and Georgina.

'Perhaps he fancied a walk on the beach and couldn't be bothered to walk along to the stone steps that led down to the sands,' thought Harriet.

Georgina and Jim were watching a big tanker on the horizon. Jim was telling Georgina about shipping routes that these tankers take to the oil refineries.

They all soon began to feel a little chilly and decided to return to the hotel. As they neared the hotel gate, Gavin came back up from the beach and climbed back over the wall, carrying nothing!

He saw them and said, 'Oops, too lazy to walk to the steps, my father was a mountain goat!' He said laughing and trotted across the road into the hotel.

Harriet said nothing.

They decided to go to their rooms and have an early night. The trauma of the day made them all feel weary. As they turned into the drive, they saw two police cars parked in the driveway. As they entered the foyer, the receptionist met them.

'I am sorry Mr Talbot and ladies, but the police have a search warrant to go through your rooms and all those on this morning's trip. If you would like to sit in the lounge until they have finished. Our manager, Mr Sparrow, is accompanying the officers.'

They walked through the lounge and decided to sit in the conservatory so they could watch the sunset. Lydia Madget was already sitting there with her knitting.

Harriet decided to tell her companions her thoughts regarding Gavin's visit to the beach.

'While you were chatting as we sat on the bench, earlier I saw Gavin Thomas climb over the wall,' she told them.

'Yes, we saw him as we walked back to the hotel,' Jim said.

'No, I saw him when he went down to the beach before that, he was carrying a black carrier bag. But when he came back up, he didn't have the bag with him! Could he have had a gun or cyanide in the bag? As he must have been warned that the police were coming to search our rooms.'

Jim hesitated before replying, 'We can't make accusations and where would he have hidden it in the café?'

Georgina said, 'I thought he was such a nice young man, why would he want to harm Mrs Rabitay? I think we should try and talk to him, to see if he knew Gert prior to coming on this trip. I still don't understand why a young man would come on this sort of coach trip with all us oldies.'

'You would be the best one to get him into conversation Georgie, he is sitting on his own in the lounge reading a book.' Harriet was peering round the curtains into the lounge.

'Now girls, the police won't take kindly to interference, but on the other hand we can't go pointing the finger at young Gavin without good reason.' Jim was trying to look severe, but the twinkle in his eye told a different story. He missed being a policeman and the intrigues of an investigation still excited him.

But he wasn't going to encourage his friends, as he knew they didn't need it, as their noses were obviously twitching in anticipation.

Georgina left the conservatory and walked towards Gavin's table.

'Hello Gavin, do you mind if I join you. It is getting a little chilly in the sun room.'

'Not at all Mrs Wright, think we could all do with some company after the day we have had. Mrs Rabitay was not the most pleasant lady and think she bullied her husband from what I could see on the bus.'

Georgina didn't want to push the subject too much but as he had mentioned Gert's name she thought it safe to proceed.

'Did you know Mrs Rabitay before you came on this trip Gavin?'

Gavin hesitated, and then shook his head, 'No I had never met either of them before.'

Georgina wasn't sure if he was telling the truth, as he looked positively uncomfortable at the question.

Gavin got up as the Inspector walked into the lounge, and announced that the room searches were complete.

'Nice to chat Mrs Wright, got to have a shower before dinner.'

With that Gavin hurried out of the lounge.

Jim and Harriet came through from the sun lounge and they all proceeded to the lift.

'Well, that young man didn't seem to want to talk, and couldn't escape quickly enough when I asked him if he knew the Rabitays before he came on the trip.'

'Did you get anything from him?' Harriet asked, as the lift ascended to their floor.

'No. Only that he said that he didn't know Gert before coming on the trip. But it wasn't very convincing.'

Gavin left the lounge not stopping to speak to the Inspector, leaving Georgina puzzled.

Harriet and Jim came over to Georgina and they all walked to the lift.

'Come in for a while, we can have a chat about today's events,' Harriet said to Jim, as she unlocked their bedroom door.

Georgina told them that, at first, Gavin was friendly.

'When I asked him if he knew Gert before, he said no, and then got up to go, but not convinced he was telling the truth.'

'What was he doing on the beach earlier? He definitely had a black carrier bag when he climbed over the wall, but when he came back, he had nothing in his hands,' Harriet said. 'We had been told about the police's intention to search our rooms before we left the hotel, so was Gavin hiding something, like a gun?'

'Or poison?' Georgina said.

'Now ladies, don't get carried away! The lad may have a perfectly good reason to take a bag to the beach. There are refuse baskets all along the beach, he may just have had some rubbish to dispose of,' Jim said, getting anxious that his friends were getting into Sherlock mode again. 'Now I think we should get ready for our dinner and perhaps take part in the quiz that is on the menu tonight after we have eaten. Leave the police to do their job.'

With that, Jim returned to his own room leaving Georgina and Harriet still puzzling over the day's events.

While Georgina was having her shower, Harriet slipped quietly out of their room and descended in the lift. She left the hotel and crossed the road and walked to the set of steps that led down to the beach, a few yards along the promenade.

She walked to the nearest refuse bin and peered inside. No sign of a plastic carrier bag. She then walked to the next two bins, but again no carrier bag.

She glanced up the bank where Gavin had descended and noticed that some of the flowers on the bank seemed disturbed. She had taken her camera with her and took a couple of snaps of the bank.

She decided that it wasn't sensible to try and climb up the bank, as Gavin had done, so she returned to the promenade by the steps she came down. She trotted back to the hotel and entered their room, just as Georgina came out of the bathroom.

Harriet went straight into the bathroom for her bath before Georgina asked her any questions.

They dressed for dinner and after they had eaten, went into the lounge and found three adjacent chairs ready for the quiz.

Everyone seemed very subdued, but the quiz master was a cheery chap and managed to make them all laugh, which was good.

No one felt like a late night, so at nine most of the guests were making for their rooms. After they exited the lift, they passed an open door which was a room in which the chamber maids kept their hoovers and cleaning equipment, they noticed that the door was open. Harriet being Harriet, looked into the room. Inside was Dennis Rabitay talking animatedly to one of the maids. Harriet dropped to her knees to pretend to tie her shoelace.

'No Lucy, I cannot do as you ask, I have to stay here!' She heard Dennis say. Harriet couldn't hover any longer outside the door, so scuttled after Jim and Georgina.

They said goodnight to Jim and went into their room.

Harriet repeated what she had heard Dennis Rabitay say to ~~Georgina~~ Lucy, but it didn't make a lot of sense to either of them. So, they decided to forget it for now and get ready for bed.

Runaway Rabbit!

The next morning, the weather was again sunny. The ladies and Jim decided, while they were having breakfast, to take the hotel minibus down into Bournemouth for the morning.

'No sign of Dennis this morning,' Jim said. 'I feel sorry for him really, perhaps we could ask him to come with us to Bournemouth.'

Both ladies agreed that it would be a nice thing to do. But by the time it was time for the minibus to depart, there was no sign of Dennis. So, they decided that he might be having a lie in and got onto the bus for their trip without him. Several other guests also got on the bus.

They spent the morning walking through the central gardens, had a coffee in one of the seaside cafes. Georgina decided she wanted to have a look in the Debenhams store, that was across the road from the café. Jim bought a newspaper and Harriet a magazine, so they enjoyed an ice cream and the views, while they waited for Georgina. Lydia Madget had hurried off by herself and the Rammidges were going to the museum.

When they arrived back at the hotel, they were surprised to see the Inspector waiting for them.

'Good morning, Jim and ladies. Mr Sparrow, the manager told us that he thought Dennis Rabitay had gone to town with you?'

'Lydia Madget and a couple more came to town, but not Dennis.'

'No Paul, we were going to invite him to come with us, but he didn't come down to breakfast and didn't appear before the minibus left,' Jim told him.

'I have been up to his room and he didn't reply, so we assumed that he was with you. Think we had better have a look in his room.

Paul Kennedy summoned the manager and requested a key to check Dennis's room. It was necessary to check that Dennis was safe.

They all followed the Inspector up in the lift along with Mr Sparrow. When they got to no 37. The Inspector told them he would deal with this and asked them to return to their own rooms.

Later, after they had deposited their coats and bags, they all agreed to meet downstairs. They ordered drinks and a took a light lunch from the buffet that the hotel laid on for their guests. As they sat in the conservatory with their food on the table beside them, Inspector Kennedy joined them. He had been invited by the manager to partake in the refreshment from the buffet.

'Do you mind if I join you? I need a chat.'

Jim pulled another chair up to their table and Paul Kennedy sat down.

'It seems that Dennis Rabitay has disappeared,' he said.

'His bed doesn't appear to have been slept in, but none of his clothes and toiletries are missing, according to one of the chambermaids who serviced the rooms on your floor. The other girl who also worked on the second floor hasn't turned up for work.'

'Is the girl that hasn't turned up to work, the dark-haired girl with a pony tail, called Lucy?' Harriet asked.

Mr Sparrow who had just brought over the coffee pot to refill Paul's cup said, 'Yes, that's right'

Paul Kennedy frowned, 'You haven't been snooping again Mrs Holt?'

'Me, Inspector? We were returning to our room last night, as we passed the cleaning ladies storeroom, I saw Dennis in there talking to someone he called Lucy. This is the second time we have overheard a conversation between Dennis and this girl. Georgina heard the first one, and we wondered then what was going on. Last night it seemed Lucy was trying to get Dennis to go somewhere with her. So perhaps she succeeded.'

Paul Kennedy looked puzzled. 'Do you know of any relationship between your chamber maid and Dennis Rabitay?' He asked hotel manager, Andrew Sparrow.

'Not to my knowledge Inspector. All I know is that Lucy's mother is quite poorly in hospital. Maybe her mother has taken a turn for the worse and Lucy has had to go to her. But she is normally very good in letting us know if she is not able to come to work.'

'I will need Lucy's address. I will send my Sergeant round to find out why she hasn't been to work.' Andrew Sparrow hurried off to his office to find Lucy's address.

'Well thank you Mrs Holt, but no more sleuthing!' He said, as his phone started to ring. He left the sun room to take the call.

The hotel manager returned looking for the Inspector, 'He is taking a phone call, leave the address on the table, as he hasn't finished his coffee so, he will return'

Mr Sparrow left the folded piece of paper on their table.

Harriet glanced at the address.

Jim cleared his throat to warn Harriet of the return of Paul Kennedy.

He sat down, finished his coffee and put the address into his pocket and then left them. They saw his car leave the hotel, blue lights flashing.

'Perhaps someone has hijacked the prime minister,' Georgina said laughing.

Harriet got out her diary and made an entry, both Jim and Georgina were aware that it was the address of the chambermaid Lucy.

'I think you should leave it to them Harriet,' Jim said.

'Oh definitely, but it could be useful, just in case!'

'It is the trip to Salisbury tomorrow, I hope the weather will be as good as today,' Jim said as he stretched his legs, 'Think l fancy a stroll along the beach, what about you ladies? There may be some shells or pretty pebbles to find.'

Both the woman thought that it would be a lovely idea. So, they left the comfort of the sun room and popped up to their rooms to fetch their coats and then strolled across the road to the steps that went down to the beach.

Harriet rolled up her trousers and decided to have a paddle. Georgina walked over to some little boys who were exploring a rock pool. She realised that these children were the twins that had been at Portland on the day Mrs Rabitay died. Jim had found a breakwater and sat watching Georgina and Harriet.

The boy's mother recognised Georgina, and asked if there was any more news about the lady who had died.

They had a little chat about the sad day, and Georgina said, 'Hope that the boys hadn't been too upset about it all.'

'No not at all, children are so resilient and I don't think they realised how serious it was. They were more upset that one of their birthday balloons had burst, and making sure that we had ice cream for tea.'

'That's good, well I had better make sure my friend doesn't fall into the water.'

Georgina wandered down to the water's edge, picking up some pretty pink shells and some small stones.

'Come on Harriet, think Jim wants to walk a little way along the beach. We will walk to the next set of steps. There is an ice cream booth along there we can sit on the promenade and enjoy our ice creams.'

They climbed back up to the promenade, found the ice cream booth and ordered three large cones and sat on the adjacent wooden bench.

There was a little breeze, but it was pleasant to just sit.

'Do you think Dennis has run off with the chambermaid or do you think he has done a bunk?' Harriet said.

'Well, if her mother is sick maybe not and Dennis didn't seem to be the sort to chase after young women,' Georgina said as she finished her ice cream.

'I think I will have a chat to young Gavin this afternoon, he was in the sun lounge reading when we came out. I just have a hunch he knows more than he is saying,' Jim said.

'Oh Jim, you keep telling us not to get involved,' Harriet said. 'I think Georgina and I are going for a bus ride this afternoon. Come along Georgie, let's get our bags, we have time to catch the hotel minibus to town.'

Georgina didn't argue, as she was aware that her friend had been quiet while on the beach.

Jim went straight into the sun room to find Gavin and the ladies hurried to the lift to collect their handbags.

When went past the reception desk, they saw Sergeant Robbins talking to Andrew Sparrow. They laid their room keys on the reception desk and looked at the brochures nearby. They clearly heard the Sergeant tell the manager that he had called at Lucy's house and had been told by her younger brother that she was at the hospital, as their mother was seriously ill. He also said that no one else had been to their house and he didn't know Dennis Rabitay.

'Do you know where we are going Harriet?'

Harriet nodded, 'I had planned to go and find Lucy but it appears to be dead end. So perhaps we can just go for a walk towards the Hengistbury Head place.'

So the ladies wandered back along the promenade, but soon realised their destination was further than they thought. So, they wandered back to the hotel and decided to sit in the hotel garden, until it got a bit chilly.

Jim met them at the lift and said he had spent the afternoon having a chat with Gavin and was now going up to his room for a nap.

As the lift door opened, Dennis Rabitay came through from the reception area and ran to the lift, before the doors closed.

'Hello Dennis, we wondered where you had gone,' Harriet said.

'Yes, sorry to disappear but I went to see an old friend in Winton. We got talking and ended up having a drink or two. So, I stayed the night on his settee'

Dennis seemed quite relaxed and his story seemed reasonable enough.

Andrew Sparrow had seen Dennis return and he immediately made a call to the Inspector's office as he had been requested.

When they got to their floor, Jim asked Dennis if he would like to join them for dinner that evening, he was quite happy to do this and told them he was going to have a shower and would meet them downstairs later for dinner.

Jim got to the dining room before the ladies and Dennis came to join him just after he had sat down.

'We are all so sorry for your loss Dennis, if there is anything we can do please don't hesitate to ask,' Jim told him.

'It is no secret that Gert could be very difficult, she always needed to be in charge. Old mother Thomas was just the same, suppose I should have been prepared. They say look at the mother and you will see the daughter in years to come! She insisted on being called Trudy, hated Gertrude!'

Just then Georgina and Harriet arrived and sat at their table. They didn't really know what to say to Dennis. Fortunately, Jim remembered his interest in photography and they discussed some of the views that Dennis had photographed.

Andrew Sparrow came into the dining room and came over to their table.

'I have had a call from Inspector Kennedy, he would like to speak to you. He is on the phone in my office.'

Dennis followed the hotel manager.

Several minutes later Dennis returned, he looked pale.

'He wants to take me back to our house in Longton and have a look round. He asked if I would agree, if I didn't, he said he could get a search warrant. What do you think Jim? I have nothing to hide, but Gert would be furious.'

'It is normal practice Dennis, and sadly Gert is in no position to make a fuss! If you like I will come with you, I wasn't keen on going to Stonehenge tomorrow anyway.' Jim looked at Harriet and Georgina, hoping they wouldn't mind.

Dennis looked relieved, 'Thanks Jim, I would appreciate your company.'

They enjoyed their food and then went into the other room and listened to the little band and even managed a little sing song.

Lydia Madget had been sharing a table with Major and Mrs Rammidges, since the girl guides had gone camping. The Major quite enjoyed having the young woman to converse with. They had also gone to listen to the music, but Mrs Rammidges soon wanted to go up to their room.

Lydia often sat in the conservatory with her knitting. Even on the trip to Portland, Lydia had taken her knitting. She had told Harriet that she knitted tiny hats for the hospital, for premature babies.

She had sat in a deck chair on the promenade in Weymouth knitting, while waiting for Bert to come back with the bus.

When the Major and his wife left, Harriet beckoned Lydia to come and join them. Dennis also said goodnight and followed the Rammidges to the lift.

'How are you getting on Lydia, are you going to Salisbury tomorrow?' Georgina asked.

'Well, I did think about going, but the Major and Felicity have decided to have a quiet day as the Major's arthritis is playing him up.'

'You are welcome to come with us Lydia, Jim is not coming with us so we could 'make it a girl's day out'.'

Lydia thanked Harriet.

'That's settled then. How are you getting on with the Rammidges?'

Lydia hesitated before replying. 'They are ok, but Felicity didn't like Mrs Rabitay at all. I was surprised when Felicity told me, when her husband went to the toilet, that Gert was not a nice person.'

'Oh really,' Georgina said, 'I didn't know that she was acquainted with the Rabitays?'

'Perhaps I shouldn't say, she told me in confidence.'

Harriet told Lydia that anything she told them would not be repeated, she did have her fingers crossed under the table!

'Apparently, Mrs Rabitay owned a fancy dress shop in Weymouth up till a year ago. Felicity went to work in the afternoons for her a few years back, as the Major was still in the army and away quite a lot. There was a bit of bother over a customer and an expensive dress and she sacked Felicity. She said it was actually Mrs Rabitays mistake but she blamed Felicity.'

'I can just imagine Gert in a fancy dress shop,' Georgina said.

'Gert called it a boutique. When the Rammidges got onto the bus she had recognised Gert straight away, but Gert didn't recognise her, or so she thought.

Quite a lot of years have passed. So, Felicity sat as far away from the Rabitays as possible.

'But at dinner on the first night, she went into the ladies' room and Gert came in. She apparently had realised who Felicity was, and made remarks like, 'I wonder what your major would say if he knew is wife was a thief'!

'Felicity was very upset, I found her crying in the sun room. She was terrified that Gert would say something to her husband, as he is a magistrate and would be horrified at any suggestion that is wife had broken the law.'

Lydia looked tearful. 'Felicity said she wished she had never come on this trip and that she would kill Gert if she said anything to her husband, but she had drunk two glasses of wine that night, so I think it was just the drink talking. But now I do wonder, do you think I should tell the police?'

Harriet took her hand and said, 'If you do and she is innocent, then the Major would find out, so perhaps for now you should just keep quiet.'

'Yes, I agree Lydia, and Felicity doesn't look like a murderer, she is very timid. Don't worry about it, the police are sorting it out,' Georgina said.

They sat and listened to the music for another half hour when Georgina said, 'If we are going out in the morning, then I need my beauty sleep.'

Harriet and Lydia also decided to go up to bed. They said goodnight to Lydia as she alighted the lift on the first floor, and agreed to meet after breakfast the next day.

When Harriet and Georgina got into their beds that night, they discussed Lydia's comments about Felicity Rammidge.

'Don't suppose she did kill Gert, do you Harry?'

'No, we all say things like that at times. I could murder Margaret Sharples at times, but no intent to actually do it.'

'But she could be another suspect I suppose, but let our mighty police force sort it out. We can always give them a hint if they are struggling.'

Harriet laughed, 'And wouldn't Paul Kennedy love that. Night, night, Georgie.'

The next morning, Dennis joined them for breakfast. Lydia sat with the Rammidges. She gave them a wave as they say down at their table.

'What time is Inspector Kennedy picking you up Dennis?' Jim asked.

'He said after breakfast, so I assume within the hour. I am all ready and I am grateful that you are coming with me. The Inspector won't object, will he?'

'No, he knows me very well and, in the circumstances, it won't be pleasant going back home on your own.'

Soon after they had finished eating, Inspector Kennedy came into the dining room holding a coffee and joined Jim and Dennis. The ladies took their drinks into the conservatory and Lydia joined them. The hotel bus was due to leave at ten.

Something Lurking in the Wood Shed

When they had finished their drinks, Dennis, Jim and Paul Kennedy left the hotel. The women watched them as they drove out of the hotel driveway.

'Poor Dennis, it will be hard to go home alone,' said Georgina.

There was little conversation in the car as they drove back to Dennis's home. He lived a few miles from Gorlstone, where Jim and the ladies lived, in small hamlet called Longton, three miles from Darrington.

When they pulled up outside his house, Dennis was concerned to see a police van with other officers already there.

'I just want to conduct a search of your property as I explained. My men will not disturb anything. I will also need to look in your outbuildings,' Paul Kennedy explained.

Dennis unlocked the front door to allow the two other police officers to enter.

Jim decided to have a walk round the front garden, while Dennis went into the house with the police officers.

Paul Kennedy advised Dennis to go and sit in the lounge, once the officers had looked round. Paul himself went back outside to look in the garden sheds and the greenhouse in the back garden.

Jim came back into the house a little later and joined Dennis in the lounge.

Dennis said, 'I could make you a cup of tea Jim, but don't know if the Inspector will allow it.'

'It's best to just stay here Dennis, and let them get on with things.'

Shortly, the Inspector came into the lounge, he had a container wrapped up in plastic bag in his hands.

'Mr Rabitay can you tell me what you had this for?'

'What is it? I don't recognise it,' Dennis said as he got up and walked towards the Inspector.

'It is potassium cyanide,' Inspector Kennedy told him. 'Have you had trouble with wasps?'

Dennis looked completely flummoxed. 'I have never seen that before and no we have never had a wasp problem. Where did you find it?'

'It was on a shelf in your garden shed. The shed was unlocked, is that usual?'

Dennis turned to Jim, 'Honestly Jim, I have never seen that before, we never lock the shed.'

'We will be taking this to our forensic department for tests. We haven't found anything else of interest. So, we will take you back to the hotel for now and will need to take a further statement from you.'

Dennis locked the house up, and all three of them returned to the police car. The Police van followed them back to Bournemouth.

Dennis turned to Jim in the car, 'I have no idea where that came from Jim. I certainly wouldn't have left the shed door unlocked with something a lethal as that inside.'

'The forensic boys will check it for fingerprints and I saw there is a label on the side giving the store where it was sold. Whoever bought it would have to sign for such a lethal chemical, so don't worry yet.'

Further conversation was muted on the journey back to the hotel.

'We will call into the station in Bournemouth, for you to add to your statement, and I will need to take you prints.'

Jim and Dennis arrived back to the hotel after the visit to the police station, just after the bus returned the ladies from their visit to Salisbury.

Jim and Dennis who hadn't eaten, went to the dining room to get lunch from the buffet. Georgina and Harriet had eaten lunch in Salisbury. Lydia had gone off on her own shopping.

They decided to wait for Jim in the sun lounge while he ate his lunch. Lydia went to her room for a lie down, she told them.

When Jim joined them, he told them that Dennis had decided to revisit his friend in Winton that afternoon but would be back in time for dinner.

Jim told Harriet and Georgina about the Inspector finding the cyanide in the Rabitay's garden shed.

'Oh lor, does that mean he could have poisoned his wife?' Georgina asked.

'He denies any knowledge of the stuff being in his shed. I almost believed him, he seemed very shocked!' Jim told them.

'The police will go to the shop where it was sold, as it clearly had a shop label on the container. They will have a signature of the purchaser as it has to be signed for.'

'I hope Dennis doesn't disappear like he did the last time he visited his friend!' Harriet said.

'The police have the address of where he went last time, so hopefully Dennis is as innocent as he states.'

Visit to Christchurch

They had bought magazines and newspapers in Salisbury and intended to spend the afternoon in the sunroom. This suited Jim, as the trip to Longton had been stressful for him and Dennis. Jim had been surprised when Dennis had decided to go to Winton for the afternoon.

Andrew Sparrow came over to ask how things had gone at Dennis's house, and then told them he was going to go to go to see his elderly aunt in Christchurch. Harriet looked interested and mentioned the old Priory there.

'Hasn't it got an interesting tale about a beam that appeared overnight?' Harriet asked.

'Yes, if you would like to come for a ride, as my aunt only lives round the corner from the Priory. My wife is coming with me and we will only be about an hour at the most, at aunt Jemima's'

Harriet looked at Georgina who told her to go, as she was feeling a little tired after walking round Salisbury all morning.

So, Harriet rushed up to the room to collect her coat and bag. Mrs Sparrow arrived at the hotel and was introduced to Harriet. She was a very friendly woman who filled Harriet in about aunt Jemima's history.

It was only a twenty minutes ride from the hotel to Christchurch. Mrs Sparrow gave Harriet directions to the Priory, when they arrived at aunt Jemima's cottage.

Harriet followed the route she had been given and rounding a corner she stopped and pulled back into a shop doorway. Dennis had just come out of an alley that led up to some cottages. A girl, who Harriet recognised as the chamber maid Lucy, walked in front of him and got into a blue ford Escort that was parked on the road. Dennis walked round to the passenger door and climbed in.

'So much for his friend in Winton,' Harriet thought.

The blue Escort drove off towards Bournemouth, Harriet stayed in the shop doorway, until they had passed her. She then continued to the Priory.

Just over half an hour later, Harriet walked back to Andrew Sparrow's car, five minutes later, Mr and Mrs Sparrow came out of their aunts cottage and they drove back to Bournemouth.

Georgina and Jim had gone up to their rooms to get ready for dinner by the time Harriet got back to the hotel.

Harriet told Georgina about seeing Dennis, and she was amazed.

'I wonder if Dennis will be back, in time for dinner as he said.'

'We will soon find out,' Harriet said.

They got dressed and met Jim outside their room and descended in the lift.

Dennis wasn't in the dining room, but Georgina caught sight of him talking to Inspector Kennedy in the reception area.

'At least he is back in the hotel. Do you think I should mention that I saw him in Christchurch?' Harriet said.

Jim was surprised as they hadn't had time to tell him.

Before they could discuss it, Dennis came and sat down looking puzzled.

'Inspector Kennedy has been to the shop where the cyanide was purchased and seen the register that was signed by the purchaser. I just don't understand it all. The register said that Gert bought the cyanide. But I swear it's not her signature. Whoever bought it gave our address and produced some form of identity. I don't understand.'

'Oh, my goodness Dennis, that is weird. Did you have a problem with wasps?'

Harriet was intrigued.

'Gert wouldn't have known what to buy or even where to get it from even if we did have a wasp problem, which we never had. But the Inspector says it was definitely a woman who bought the cyanide. They are trying to get some security camera film from the street outside.'

As dinner was served, they tried to get their heads around the latest information. Each of them had their own thoughts.

'The police will hopefully get some pictures of the woman then they will see if it was Gert. Try not to worry Dennis,' Jim said.

After the meal, Dennis said he was going to have an early night, the ladies and Jim took their coffee into the sun room.

'Look girls, I think it's time we came clean to the Inspector. I know he won't be too impressed by interference, but we have seen things that should be reported for him to investigate.' Jim was looking very serious.

'I think we should pool our observations,' Harriet said.

'Firstly, why was Gavin and Gert having words on our first night, then an hour before the police were going to search our rooms, he took something down onto the beach and got rid of it?'

Georgina interrupted Harriet, 'I have been thinking about the supposed gun shot. This is only a wild guess but when we went paddling on the beach, remember I told you I saw that family with the twins who had been at Portland the day that Gert was killed. The mother told me that the twins weren't upset by the events of that day, they were more upset that one of their birthday balloons had burst. So, what if there was no gun just a balloon bursting? Gert just had a hissy fit; she was a drama queen.'

'That is very plausible Georgie, why don't I just ask Gavin what he took down to the beach?' Harriet said.

'I haven't been quite honest with you girls. When you told me that Gert's maiden name was Thomas, it made me think. Gavin told me that he now worked for the Dorset Echo. I phoned up an old mate of mine yesterday who is a sub editor on the paper and asked him if he knew Gavin. What he told me, made me wonder if he did have a motive to kill Gert. He phoned me back half an hour ago.

'Gavin's mother was Gert Rabitay's sister, a fact that he has kept quiet about. John told me that Gavin went through a bad time several years ago. His grandmother died ten years ago, and Alice, Gavin's mother had moved in with her and looked after her for several years. When she became ill, Gert got back in contact and persuaded her mother to leave everything to her.

'When his grandmother died, Gavin's mother had to move out of her mother's house, Gert gave her sister nothing. She set up the dress shop up in Weymouth and left her sister relying on Gavin to support her. Gavin hated her.'

'So, Gavin did have a reason to kill Gert,' Georgina said.

'Oh, what tangled webs we weave!' Harriet said. 'We have Dennis acting strangely, and Gavin having reason to hate Gertrude, and Felicity scared out of her wits in case Gert may have told her husband about her indiscretion.'

They all sat and mulled over events and realised Jim was right they should have a word with Inspector Kennedy.

'Just to change the subject,' Georgina said. 'I want to go out into the hotel gardens before we leave on Saturday. They have a highly scented viburnum out there, and I want to borrow a few cuttings!'

She got up and left the sun room, leaving her companions still thinking over the murder.

As Georgina went down the stone steps into the hotel gardens, she saw Lucy sitting on a stone bench having a cigarette.

'Hello Lucy, how is your mother? I hear she has been poorly!'

Lucy smiled and moved along the seat for Georgina to sit down beside her.

'She is doing fine now, but it was touch and go for a few days. But, at last, everything is turning around and life is looking good. They say things come in threes. My mum getting back to rights, and now Mr Sparrow has just offered me a permanent job here.'

'That's great Lucy, you like your job here then?'

'Mr Sparrow said in the winter months when we are quiet, he would like to train me up for a job on reception for next year.'

'You said that three good things have happened Lucy?' Georgina asked.

'Yes, everything seems to be sorting itself out. I shouldn't really say any more…

Jim and Harriet decided that the following day they would take a taxi down to Bournemouth police station and have a chat with Inspector Kennedy.

They then went to the lift instead of getting in with Jim, Harriet told Jim that she would go and find Georgina in the gardens before going up to her room. She waited till the doors on the lift had closed, and she went out of the front door of the hotel and went down the drive and crossed the road.

The sun was just about setting, but there was enough light for Harriet to climb over the wall as Gavin had done. She slithered down the bank…

Georgina entered the hotel with her 'borrowed' cuttings inside her cardigan, and made for the lift. As the lift doors were just closing, four girls along with Miss Jones rushed into the lift.

'We are sleeping in the hotel tonight, but we have been sleeping in our tents on Robinson Crusoe's Island,' one of the girls told Georgina.

'I am sorry about the girls, they have been so excited. We did have fun, didn't we girls? We are going home on Friday and decided to have our last night in the hotel.'

Georgina laughed, 'I used to be a girl guide many years ago, but I never went camping, you are lucky. Did you see any of the red squirrels on the island?'

As the lift got to the first floor, the girls seemed reluctant to stop talking about their experiences. Georgina pushed the button to hold the lift doors open while the girls told her about the deer they saw.

'Come along girls you all have to have a bath and then we can eat the sandwiches that the hotel has put in our rooms.'

The girls went off to their rooms and Georgina was able to let the lift take her to the next floor.

She was surprised not to find Harriet in their room, but thought that she must still be downstairs chatting to Jim. She had a quick wash, put her nightdress on and decided to have a read of her book.

Within minutes she had dropped off to sleep.

Harriet had managed to get back up the bank. Her knees were muddy and she made sure no one was walking along the promenade, before she attempted to climb over the wall.

When she got up to their room, she was disappointed to find Georgina fast asleep. So, she crept into the bathroom and stripped off and washed the mud off, put her pyjamas on and got into bed. It wasn't long before she went to sleep.

Georgina overslept the next morning, she was surprised to see that Harriet had already gone down to breakfast. She quickly dressed and hurried down to the dining room.

Jim was already eating his breakfast but Harriet was nowhere to be seen.

'Where is Harry, Jim?'

Jim grinned and told her that Harriet had eaten her breakfast and was now in the sun room talking to Gavin Thomas. 'In Sherlock mode, I am afraid.'

'I also have some news Jim,' Georgina told him.

Jim looked heavenward and sighed.

Sergeant Robbins came into the dining room, and came over to Jim and Georgina. 'The guvnor sent me to pick you and the Miss Marples up Jim.'

'Yes, I phoned him last night and told him we needed a chat.'

The Sergeant laughed and said, 'I hope the old dears haven't been climbing out of windows again.' Georgina blushed.

Harriet joined them and after fetching their coats and bags, they followed Sergeant Robbins to his car. Fortunately, it was an unmarked police car.

On arrival at the police station, they were surprised to see Dennis being taken into an interview room, accompanied by a police officer.

The Sergeant took Jim and the ladies along a corridor to Inspector Kennedy's office.

He shook Jim's hand and indicated two chairs to Harriet and Georgina.

'Why is Dennis here, Inspector?' Georgina asked.

'He is being interviewed again about the murder of his wife! We found cyanide at his home and he is refusing to say where he went on the night after his wife's death. We believe another woman is involved.'

Georgina stood up and started talking. 'No, you have got this all wrong. Dennis didn't kill his wife. We told you about seeing him talking to one of the chamber maids but we got it all wrong. Harriet saw Dennis in Christchurch with Lucy the chambermaid, which added to our suspicions.

'I talked to Lucy last night. She told me that when she saw the list of incoming guests, she recognised Dennis's name. It is an unusual name. Her mother brought her up on her own and only recently told Lucy the name of her father. He was her mother's first boyfriend and the love of her life. They had an argument when Alice, Lucy's mother saw him kissing another girl. They went their separate ways but soon after found out that she was pregnant.

'Dennis had moved away after the argument heart-broken, leaving no forwarding address. Lucy's mother was in hospital, seriously ill with pneumonia, and Lucy wanted to speak to Dennis. At first, she said he didn't believe her, so she asked him to go to the hospital with her to see her mother. He stayed all night at the hospital with Lucy and thankfully Alice's condition improved.'

'That only gives him more of a motive to get rid of his wife,' Sergeant Robbins said.

Georgina had to agree, but still didn't believe that Dennis was a murderer.

'But he didn't find out about his daughter till after Gert was dead. Have you found out who the woman was who bought the cyanide?' Harriet asked.

'We will need to speak to the daughter, and we are still waiting to see the CCTV film that was taken at the shop where the poison was bought,' Sergeant Robbins said.

'Oh, my goodness we haven't helped Dennis at all,' Georgina said.

'What about Gavin Thomas?' Jim said. 'I found out that Mrs Rabitay's maiden name was Thomas. He didn't tell you that did he Paul? I also found out that Gert persuaded to her aunt to leave all her money and house to her, in her will. Instead of leaving it to Gavin's mother, as she had promised. Gavin's mother had been looking after her aunt for years. Gavin hated Gert. Harriet saw them having words on our first night.'

'Have you considered Mrs Rammidges?' Georgina said. 'She said she wished Gert was dead. She worked in Gert's posh dress shop and was fired on a trumped-up accusation of stealing. Gert taunted Felicity Rammidge in the ladies' toilet on our first night. Felicity was very upset and worried that Gert was going to tell the Major, who is, as you know, a magistrate and a stickler for honesty,' Georgina told Inspector Kennedy.

'Well, it was a woman who bought the poison, we may see when the film arrives at the station,' Paul Kennedy said.

Harriet looked at Jim and said, 'Jim, I don't think it was Gavin. You know I saw him take something down to the beach which made us suspicious, especially as the Inspector was about to search our rooms. Last night, before it got dark, I climbed over the wall across the road and clambered down the bank.'

Inspector Kennedy held his head and said, 'At least it wasn't a window!'

Harriet ignored him.

'I found a small box half hidden in the flowers with a stone with writing on. But as it was getting dark and I hadn't got my glasses I couldn't read the inscription…I managed to get back up the bank and this morning I asked Gavin about it.

'He told me that the box contained his mother's ashes. She had asked to be placed near the beach on the east cliff, so that she could see the Purbecks and the Isle of White. This was the only reason he was on the coach trip. As his car was off the road and his mother wanted to be placed there on her birthday, which was the day I saw him. He was horrified to find that Mrs Rabitay was on the coach trip, and he had bumped into her when he was looking over the wall on our first day. He was deciding the best place to put her ashes. He said he couldn't resist having a go at her, but swore he hadn't killed her, and I believe him.'

'We are certainly gathering suspects,' Paul Kennedy said.

'Did Mrs Rammidge tell you herself about Gert's insinuations,' Paul asked Harriet.

'No, it was Miss Madget. She has been sitting on the Rammidges' table since the girl guides went camping, and got friendly with Felicity Rammidges. She said she found Felicity crying in the sun room.'

'So, Mrs Rammidges hasn't told anyone else about it, I think I had better have another chat with her.' The Inspector nodded to his Sergeant who was taking notes of the conversation.

'Well, the Miss Marples been in action, but it seems to have only muddied the waters, and we just seem to have made matters worse,' Harriet said.

Jim said, 'I was wondering if this could be something you should follow up Paul. When I went to Dennis's house with you, I went out into the front garden. The old biddy next door was cutting the privet in between her garden and the Rabitays. She was obviously ear wigging and trying to see what was going on. So, I had a chat with her.

'She obviously wasn't a fan of Gertrude. She told me that the Rabitays had fostered a couple of girls before she bought the dress shop. 'She was always shouting at the girls', the woman told me. Then one of them got herself into trouble, shoplifting she said. A day or so later one of the girls wasn't there anymore. She did wonder where she had gone. Gert had told her that she had been taken back into care. The other girl had looked dreadful after the other one had gone, and a week later, she went as well. That what she told me. Then Gert's aunt had died, and she had bought the shop in Weymouth.

'Then the woman told me that she had seen a woman going into the Rabitay's. She told me that she called over the fence and told her that the Rabitays were away on holiday. Apparently, the woman told her that she was just delivering a card for Gert, but the woman said she thought it was odd, as Gert's birthday was in March. But she said her son had turned up with her grandchildren, so she didn't see the woman leave, and didn't think any more about it.'

'I think you will have to take a drive down to Longton, Sergeant, sooner rather than later. See if you can get a description of the visitor to the Rabitay's home. Also call into Palmouth police station on your way back and see George Reynolds, the station Sergeant, and get him to check the records about any girls booked for shop lifting. You will have to go back at least ten years as Mrs R had the dress shop for about eight years, so had to be before that.'

Sergeant Robbins grabbed his coat and appeared not too happy at having to drive to Longton.

'Which neighbour was it Jim?'

'The one on the right, as you look at Rabitays, it's a white gabled place,' Jim told him.

'Well Jim and ladies, we will look into your observations.' With that, the Inspector ushered them out of the station and instructed a lady constable to drive them back to their hotel.

At the Police Station

Inspector Paul Kennedy and Sergeant Clive Robbins decide it was time to reassess the case.

'Those old ladies seem once again to have unravelled information that we didn't,' Paul said.

'Nosey old bats, we ought to lock them up!' Clive said laughing.

'Well let's get down to it then. We have the husband who was obviously bullied by his old lady. And the cyanide was in his shed. But if what Miss Marple says is true, then he knew nothing about his daughter or her mother till after Mrs R was dead. But then he may have reached the end of his tether any way. He did say that he had thought about going to live with his brother and be able to go fishing when he wanted…We haven't got that CCTV film yet, what is the hold up with that?' Paul picked up the phone and spoke to the station Sergeant, and asked him to chase up the security film from the store that sold the cyanide.

'Gavin Thomas didn't tell us he was related to Mrs Rabitay, why? He must have hated her. His mother ended up homeless and didn't get the legacy that she had been promised. I think he is a probable, but who did he get to pick up the poison? As the guy in the store insists it was a female,' Clive said.

'I called in to see George Reynolds in Palmouth police station. He didn't need much of a reminder about the youngsters that had been fostered by the Rabitays. He said it played on his mind for years. It was about ten years ago.

'The girl, Lorna Paget, was picked up in Tesco's stealing cans of Coke and chocolate bars, as Mrs Rabitay wouldn't allow them the eat 'rubbish foods' as she called them. They took Lorna back home to Mrs Rabitay, she was furious. They had turned up in squad car and she was more concerned about the neighbours seeing them at her house. She yelled at Lorna, paid for the goods that she had taken, and told them to leave. Tesco had told us, that as long as the goods were paid for, and since it was her first offence, they wouldn't take any further action. Oh, she was lucky, Tesco usually get shop lifters charged,' Sergeant Robbins said.

'But the matter didn't end there. The next day, they were called to the school that the girls attended. They had found Lorna in the toilets; she had taken an overdose. According to her sister Linda, Mrs Rabitay had screamed abuse at Lorna and then sent her to bed with no dinner. She had told Lorna that she was a thief and she was going to send her back unto care.

'Sadly, they couldn't save Lorna, poor little tyke. She had taken a handful of Mrs R's sleeping tablets and paracetamol. Her sister was devastated and within a day or so Mrs Rabitay had asked the social services to remove the sister, and she went back into the care system. That was sad, the sister would be about twenty-two now. Wonder where she is?' Sergeant Robbins said.

'Felicity Rammidges was scared stiff Gert was going to spill the beans to her husband, or so the Madget woman said. Think we must speak to Mrs Rammidges tomorrow.' Inspector Kennedy was writing down notes.

Just then there was a knock on his office door and the station Sergeant came in with a package.

'The film from the security camera guv, the wife just brought it in. She has had it in her car for a couple of days, she said she had forgotten about it!'

He laid the package on the Inspectors desk, 'I will go and set the room up for you to play it!'

'We will do that now, then we will go to the hotel to see our suspects again, hopefully we can sort this out as the group are going home tomorrow.'

They picked up the film and followed the station Sergeant to view the film…

Jim, Harriet and Georgina had been for a walk along the beach to the ice cream hut, and sat on the promenade discussing events.

They felt that they may have muddied the waters regarding Gareth and Felicity, but found it hard to actually agree on who they thought was the murderer.

They had a quiet lunch from the buffet and took their coffee into the sun room. They planned to have an hour or so there, and then went to start packing their suitcases ready for their departure the next day.

Major Rammidge had gone up to his room after lunch as, 'he had made a pig of himself', according to Felicity. So she came and joined them and was doing the Times crossword sitting in a corner of the sun room.

Sergeant Robbins came into the sun room.

'Good morning, all. Mrs Rammidge, could I have a word please?'

Felicity looked up from her crossword, 'Good morning, Sergeant. Come and sit over here, it's very comfortable.'

'Perhaps you would prefer to talk to me in private, Mrs Rammidge.'

Felicity laughed, 'You are not going to arrest me, are you? These are my friends so come and sit down.' She patted the chair next to her and the Sergeant did as he was told.

'I just wanted to ask you about your relationship with Mrs Rabitay. We understand that you once worked in her dress shop.'

Felicity didn't seem fazed by the question.

'While my husband was still in the army, I got fed up with being home alone. I saw an ad in her shop window for a part time sales lady. I took the job for three afternoons a week. She was a tarter to work for, but I enjoyed talking to the customers. I stuck it for about two months.'

'We understand that there was an accusation made by Mrs Rabitay, that you stole from her?'

Felicity laughed, 'Yes, she did try that, but I proved that the missing cash was down to her not me. She refused to admit she had made the mistake. But fortunately, I found the till receipts. Whoever served a customer had to put in their own code in the till and the till receipts clearly showed that Gert had sold this particular dress. She had put in an extra digit making the price of the garment £175 not £75, so obviously the money in the till was down. She got herself into a right paddy, called me a thief, until I threatened to take her to court for defamation of character.'

'We understood that Mrs Rabitay upset you in the ladies' room on the first night of your holiday and you confided in another member of the party?'

'Oh yes, I did tell Lydia as she came into the ladies after Gert had gone, but she didn't really upset me. She had gone out in a huff; I told her that I had told Herbert all about it, and that he was a magistrate and happy to take her to court if she persisted. We had a laugh about it, as don't think Lydia liked her either.'

Harriet looked puzzled. She had heard all of the conversation but said nothing.

Jim and Georgina had also listened and looked at each other in amazement.

Inspector Kennedy had gone to speak to the hotel manager while his Sergeant was interviewing Felicity. He then came into the sun room and beckoned Jim to follow him.

'Jim, I have got the film from the shop where the poison was bought. Clive went over to see the Rabitay's neighbour and got a description of the female who visited the Rabitay's house, the day after Mrs R was murdered. The description seems very similar to the person on the security film. I was wondering if you would have a look at the film and see if you recognise her?'

'Of course, no problem. But think it might be an idea to let Harriet and Georgina see it as well. I know its irregular, but women sometimes see things we might miss.'

The Inspector thought for a moment and then agreed.

Jim called the ladies and explained the situation. They were excited.

They all got settled down in the darkened room, ready to see the security film.

They all sat quietly, and on the screen, they saw clearly a person entering the shop. The person was slight and had a jacket on with the hood covering the head. The day was very sunny and they also wore large sun glasses.

The person spoke with a slight Scottish accent, obviously a female voice. 'Been asked to get this to get rid of mother's wasps.'

She produced a piece of paper with the name of the required poison. The manager of the store told her she would have to produce proof of her name and address and sign the poison register. The woman offered a driving licence and then signed the register, then placed the bottle into a bag and then left.

'Can I see the last bit again?' Georgina asked.

Both Harriet and Georgina gasped. They both knew who the person was.

'Have you got the description of the person the neighbour saw?' Harriet asked.

Sergeant Robbins read out the description he had taken from the neighbour.

'Did the woman carry a bag when she went to the Rabitays house?' Georgina asked.

'Think she did say something about a bag.' The Sergeant got out his notes.

'Yes, the neighbour did say she was carrying a light brownish bag.'

At that moment Lydia came into the sun room with her knitting.

Harriet looked at Jim, and nodded towards Lydia. The Inspector noticed the look and then saw the canvas bag under Lydia's arm.

'Miss Madget, we are needing another word regarding the murder of Mrs Rabitay.'

Lydia turned and ran out of the sunroom.

Later that evening, as the three of them were sitting down to their meal, Jim got a phone call from Bournemouth Police station. He got up from the table and was away for about ten minutes.

When he returned, he told them that Lydia Madget, or Linda Paget as they had discovered who she really is, has been charged with the murder of Gertrude Rabitay. Apparently, she eventually admitted it. It was revenge for Gert's treatment of her and her sister and the suicide of her sister. She told the Inspector that she had gone to the Rabitay's house and put the cyanide into Dennis's shed and caught the bus back to Bournemouth in time to catch the hotel mini bus.

'So, girls you've done it again!'

They all felt it was a very sad story but were glad it was all sorted out.

Dennis joined them at their table. He had also received a call from the Inspector.

'Those two girls were never made welcome in our house, I tried to get Gert to be kinder to them, she was never cut out to be a mother.'

The following morning, they all climbed onto the bus to go home.

Dennis going home to organise his wife's funeral, but now had contact with his daughter and whatever the future had in store for him and her mother.

Inspector Kennedy had told Jim, that him and Sergeant Robbins were returning to Palmouth that day as well.

They all felt a little subdued. But the chattering girl guides on the bus lightened the mood a little.

'Dino and your doggies will be delighted to see us. I phoned Janie up last night to see if they were all behaving themselves. Apparently, Janie her boyfriend and little Teddy, have all have been staying at mine along with your pooches. She said that Dino is in charge, and thoroughly enjoying having the dogs there.'

Harriet worried about the dog's hairs and paw prints all over Georgina's immaculate kitchen. But Georgina soon put her mind at rest.

'If Dino is happy, then I am happy. Nothing that a hoover and a bit of Flash in a bucket won't clean up.'

The journey home was completed in just over an hour, the traffic had been light.

Glad to be home again, Harriet dumped her case at her front door and trotted after Georgina to collect her dogs.

Two weeks later Georgina, Harriet and Jim drove down to Darrington church for Gertrude Rabitay's funeral.

They had phoned Dennis in the week, and were pleased to hear that Lucy had taken a week's holiday to help her father organise the funeral.

When they arrived at the church, they saw Major Rammidge and Felicity getting out of their car. They exchanged greetings and went into the church.

Just before the cortege arrived, Gareth Thomas entered the church. He sat down next to Jim. Inspector Kennedy followed the coffin into the church and sat down behind them.

'I know she wasn't my favourite person, but my mother would have wanted me to pay my respects for her,' Gavin told Jim.

The funeral and interment were over fairly quickly. Afterwards, Dennis told them that a few refreshments had been prepared in the Old Oak Pub, a few doors away from the graveyard.

A couple of neighbours and the group from the holiday trip were the only ones to go to the pub.

Dennis came and thanked them all for coming. He told Jim that he was going to put the house in Longton on the market and Lucy was looking out for a bungalow near Christchurch for him.

Harriet, Jim and Georgina said goodbye to Dennis and wished him well and left.

'I suppose we will have to plan our next adventure,' Harriet said.

'The next adventure is going to be planning young Janie's wedding,' Jim told them. 'And I am going to keep a tight rein on the both of you.'